# STAR WARS®

## THE CLONE WARS™
### INCREDIBLE VEHICLES

# STAR WARS

## THE CLONE WARS™
# INCREDIBLE VEHICLES

Illustrated by Richard Chasemore • Written by Jason Fry

# CONTENTS

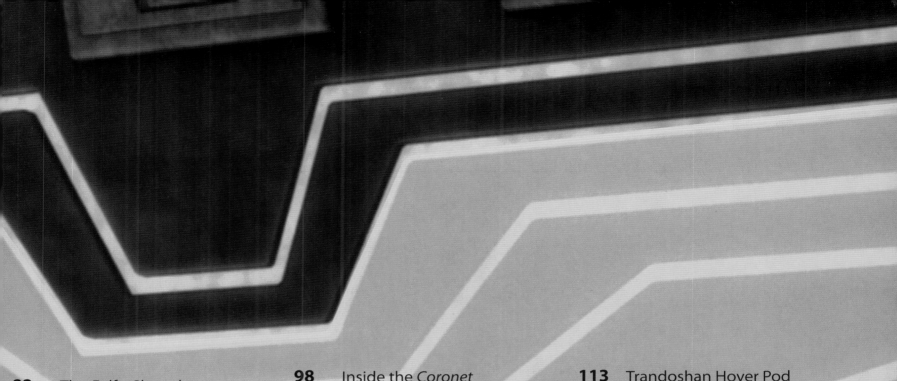

# INTRODUCTION

The Galactic Republic is in turmoil, locked in a savage civil war with the Separatist movement which has formed from breakaway star systems and greedy corporations.

The creation of a centralized Republic military after centuries of peace has driven rapid changes in vehicle design and technology, with military contractors creating new warships, assault craft, and ground vehicles by the millions for the Republic. Separatist corporations and worlds are busy too, producing cheap and deadly droid armies and adapting classes of commercial ships into mass-produced military vessels.

The war effort is driving experiments with new weapons, defenses, and communications technologies, as well as the production of sleek, deadly new starfighters and hulking capital ships, including the largest vessels seen on the spacelanes in thousands of years. Meanwhile, civilian ships of all types—private sloops, dingy freighters, and illegally modified pirate craft—continue to travel between the stars, seeking profit or merely survival in a war-torn galaxy.

# REPUBLIC WARSHIPS

TO FREE A Separatist-held planet, the Republic relies upon large warships that can descend from space to engage enemies in aerial combat, deliver clone troopers to the battlefield, and provide covering fire for ground forces as they advance on Separatist positions.

Ball turrets can fire above and below wing

## SEE ALSO

JEDI CRUISER
Pages 56–57

CONSULAR-CLASS CRUISER
Pages 10–11

PELTA-CLASS FRIGATE
Pages 20–21

STEALTH SHIP
Pages 12–13

## Assault Gunship

GUNSHIPS FERRY CLONES into combat and rake ground forces with cannons, missiles, and rockets. Troopers often give their gunships nicknames—one with a snarling wampa painted on the nose is affectionately called the "Wampa Runner."

### DATA FILE

MANUFACTURER: Rothana Heavy Engineering

MODEL: LAAT/i Repulsorlift Gunship

CLASS: Gunship

LENGTH: 17.69m (58ft)

CREW: 4

WEAPONS: Laser Cannons, Missile Launchers, Air-to-air Rockets

AFFILIATION: Republic

### DATA FILE

MANUFACTURER: Rothana Heavy Engineering

MODEL: LAAT/c Repulsorlift Gunship

CLASS: Gunship

LENGTH: 28.82m (94.5ft)

CREW: 1

WEAPONS: Laser Cannons

AFFILIATION: Republic

Wampa artwork: Many gunships have unique nose art paid for by troopers

## Republic Dropship

DROPSHIPS LACK THE troop compartments and heavy weaponry of gunships so they rely instead on brave pilots to drop off or pick up AT-TEs, artillery, and other Republic groundcraft.

AT-TE walker ready for unloading

Tail houses critical systems and is a vulnerable spot in design

Main bridge and operations stations

### Striking From Above

Assault ships are designed to transport troops to planetary surfaces, but they are also used to bombard enemy fortifications from orbit, inflicting terrible damage from space with turbolaser blasts and proton torpedoes.

### Making Planetfall

Most warships of this size never leave space, but the assault ship can land on its trio of massive landing pads and deploy ramps so that troops and groundcraft can disembark directly onto the battlefield.

Hatch to hangar for shuttles and visiting craft

## DATA FILE

MANUFACTURER: Rothana Heavy Engineering

MODEL: *Acclamator*-class Military Transport

CLASS: Heavy Cruiser

LENGTH: 891.59m (2,925ft)

CREW: 700

WEAPONS: Turbolasers, Laser Cannons, Missile/Torpedo Launch Tubes

AFFILIATION: Republic

# Republic Assault Ship

THESE GIANT TROOPSHIPS first saw action at the Battle of Geonosis. They carry gunships, walkers, speeders, and of course clone troopers to the front lines for the dangerous business of retaking another world from the Separatists.

# FRIGATE (MODIFIED)

DURING THE Clone Wars, firepower was badly needed so the Supreme Chancellor contracted the Corellian Engineering Corporation to upgrade consular ships. These graceful ships had been used for centuries by ambassadors and diplomats, but now they bristle with cannons and serve as frigates on the front lines.

## DATA FILE

MANUFACTURER: Corellian Engineering Corporation

MODEL: *Consular*-class Cruiser (retrofitted)

CLASS: Frigate

LENGTH: 139m (455ft)

CREW: 8

WEAPONS: Turbolasers, Point-defense Laser Cannons

AFFILIATION: Republic

Deflector shield generator

Turbolaser mount added in retrofit

## Seeing Red

THE SCARLET MARKINGS of consular ships once announced that a ship was on a diplomatic mission and should have safe passage through combat zones. Now that the starships are warships, red is used as a Republic Navy color.

# EMERGENCY ESCAPE POD

ALTHOUGH STATISTICS SHOW that space travel is very safe, accidents do happen: Uncharted navigational hazards, pirate attacks, or malfunctions can leave a ship helpless in deep space. Because of this, all large starships carry escape pods that have communications gear, beacons, and limited maneuvering abilities.

## DATA FILE

MANUFACTURER: Corellian Engineering Corporation

MODEL: *Consular*-class Cruiser Escape Pod

CLASS: Escape Pod

LENGTH: 9.29m (30.42ft)

CREW: 5 passengers

WEAPONS: None

AFFILIATION: Varies

*Thrusters offer limited maneuverability*

*Multi-spectrum lamps for maximum visibility*

## Quick Getaway

SOME ESCAPE PODS are luxurious mini-craft meant to offer wealthy travelers maximum comfort in an emergency. But most are simple capsules designed for hasty departures.

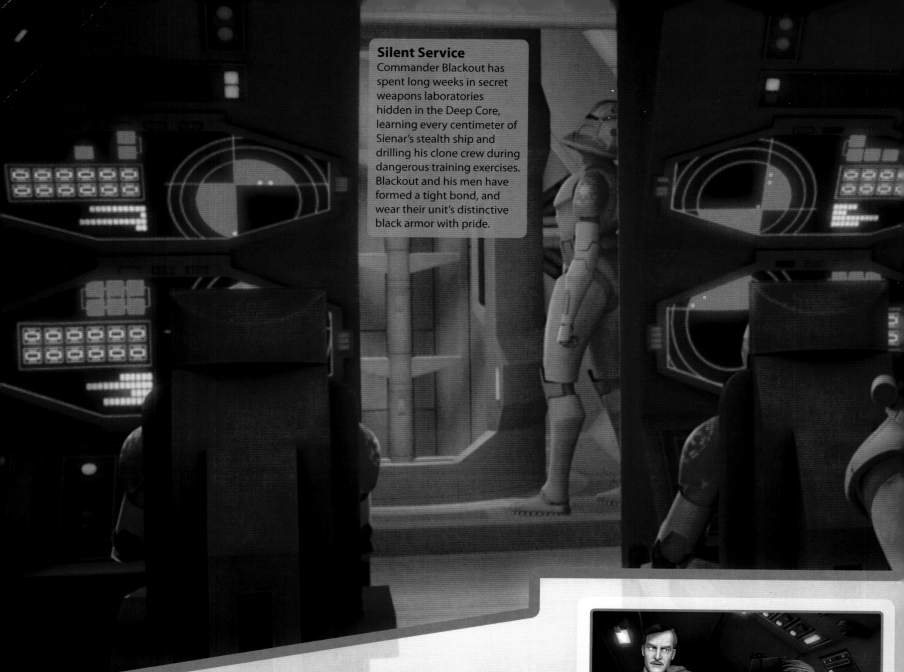

# STEALTH SHIP

AN EXPERIMENTAL VESSEL, the Republic's stealth ship uses a cloaking device—a piece of rare, expensive technology—to make it invisible to the eye and to most scanners. The stealth ship doesn't have powerful weapons, but the idea is that it shouldn't need them: Its cloaking device should allow it to slip through Separatist fleets and even blockades, gathering valuable intelligence about the enemy and delivering clone troopers for strategic strikes on enemy positions.

**Admiral and General**
Admiral Yularen admires Anakin Skywalker's courage and unerring instincts in battle, but the Jedi General has never faced the fiendish Admiral Trench during wartime. Yularen decides to accompany Anakin as he tries to slip past Trench's blockade of Christophsis for the stealth ship's first field test.

Bow enclosure houses
cloaking device

## DATA FILE

**MANUFACTURER:** Sienar Design Systems

**MODEL:** [Classified]

**CLASS:** Corvette

**LENGTH:** 99.71m (327ft)

**CREW:** 12

**WEAPONS:** Torpedo Launchers, Point-defense Laser Cannons

**AFFILIATION:** Republic

Aft point-defense
laser emplacement

Cloaking projectors
emit distortion field

Ventral sensor suite
and rectenna

### Secrecy in a Small Package

Cloaking devices were once common in the galaxy, but are now rare—limited by both their enormous cost and their large size. But the weapons makers at Sienar have figured out how to miniaturize the technology so a relatively small vessel can be cloaked.

### An Old Enemy

A veteran of many wars, Admiral Trench is now a Separatist commander. Famously aggressive, the multi-legged Harch is happiest surrounded by laserfire. Yularen fought Trench years ago at the terrible Battle of the Malastare Narrows. Trench was declared dead, but the tough old spider somehow survived.

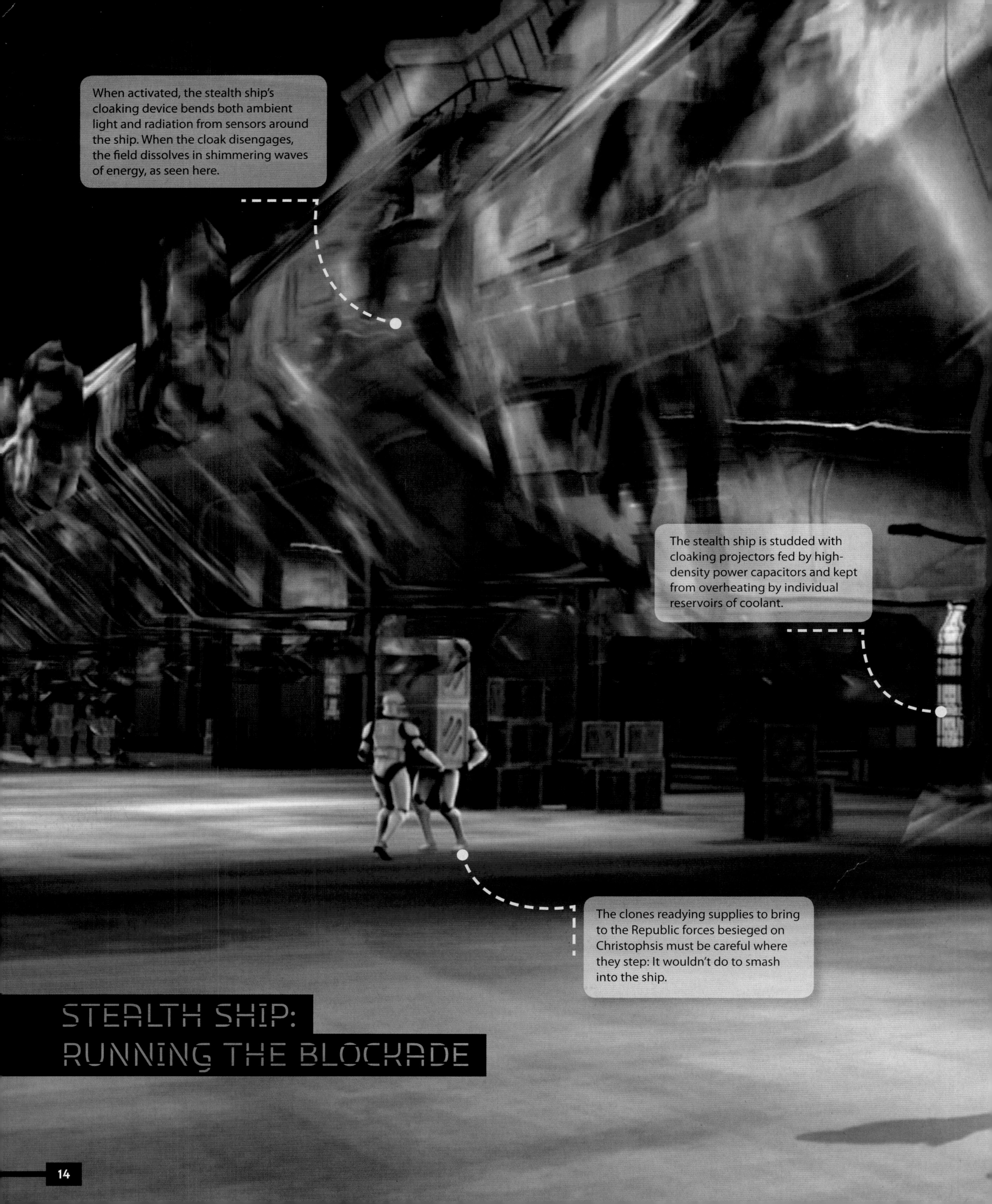

When activated, the stealth ship's cloaking device bends both ambient light and radiation from sensors around the ship. When the cloak disengages, the field dissolves in shimmering waves of energy, as seen here.

The stealth ship is studded with cloaking projectors fed by high-density power capacitors and kept from overheating by individual reservoirs of coolant.

The clones readying supplies to bring to the Republic forces besieged on Christophsis must be careful where they step: It wouldn't do to smash into the ship.

# STEALTH SHIP: RUNNING THE BLOCKADE

# Now You See It...

SENATOR BAIL ORGANA is trapped on the planet Christophsis by Admiral Trench's Separatist blockade. Anakin Skywalker wants to try a frontal assault, but Obi-Wan Kenobi has a better idea: use the Republic's experimental stealth ship to slip through the enemy lines and rescue Organa.

Annoyed at being ordered to break off his attack on the Christophsis blockade, Anakin demands to see Obi-Wan's new toy, but all he sees is an empty hangar. "Two steps forward and you'd actually be kissing it," says Obi-Wan.

# Y-Wing Fighter

MUCH ADMIRED FOR the sleek lines of its hull, the Y-wing serves the Republic as both a starfighter and a bomber. Other fighters are faster or more maneuverable, but few can take as much damage—or pack such a punch.

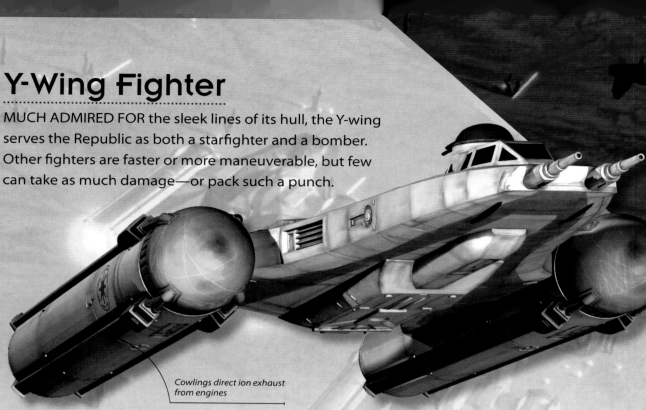

*Cowlings direct ion exhaust from engines*

## DATA FILE

MANUFACTURER: Koensayr Manufacturing

MODEL: BTL-B Y-wing Starfighter

CLASS: Starfighter

LENGTH: 23.04m (75.58ft)

CREW: 2

WEAPONS: Laser Cannons, Ion Cannons, Proton Torpedoes

AFFILIATION: Republic

**In the Shop**
Crews complain that the Y-wing's fragile systems need constant maintenance and are hard to access, forcing them to remove body panels after most missions.

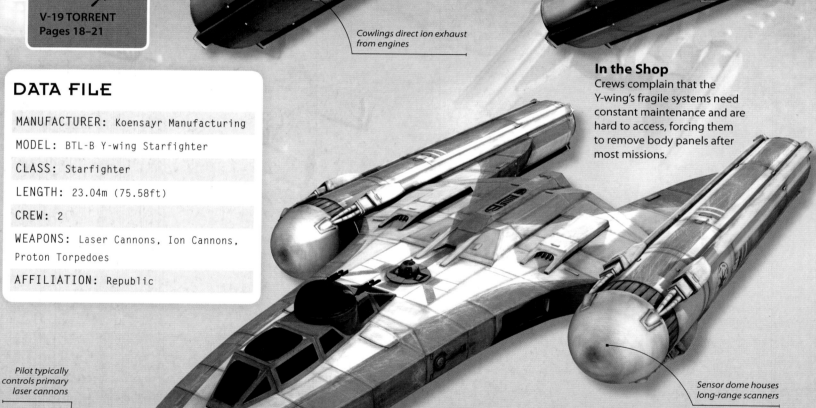

*Pilot typically controls primary laser cannons*

*Sensor dome houses long-range scanners*

**Two-man Crew**
At Kaliida Nebula, Anakin Skywalker leads Shadow Squadron in its attack on General Grievous's dreaded flagship, the *Malevolence*. While Anakin flies, Ahsoka Tano serves as her Master's gunner.

# REPUBLIC FIGHTERS

BIGGER DOESN'T ALWAYS mean better and sometimes small, speedy fighters are what a combat mission needs. Unlike heavy warships, they excel at swarming the defenses of enemy capital ships, making bombing runs against dug-in ground forces, and dueling other fighters.

*Split wings aid shielding and help shed waste heat*

*Sensor jammer housed beneath armored nose*

## DATA FILE

MANUFACTURER: Incom/Subpro

MODEL: ARC-170 Starfighter

CLASS: Starfighter

LENGTH: 12.7m (42ft)

CREW: 3

WEAPONS: Laser Cannons, Proton Torpedoes

AFFILIATION: Republic

## ARC-170 Fighter

A RUGGED FIGHTER outfitted with powerful laser cannons, the ARC-170 is equipped with a hyperdrive. This means that squadrons of ARC-170s can pursue missions on their own without relying on a carrier for transport through hyperspace, which gives Republic strategists greater flexibility.

*Cannons can batter down even capital-ship shields*

**Target: Malastare**
Squadrons of Y-wings, ARC-170s, and V-19s turn the tide in the Battle of Malastare when they bombard a Separatist army, dropping an electro-proton bomb designed to disable mechanicals without harming living beings.

## Learning Curve

THE INSECTOID VERPINE engineers who designed the V-19 built it so it could be flown with its wings in many different configurations. This gives the pilot more options, but requires more extensive training.

FRONT VIEW

### Revised Design

In Slayn & Korpil's initial V-19 design, the fighter rotated around a fixed cockpit. But the company scrapped the idea in favor of a hinged ventral wing that swings up and locks behind the cockpit for takeoffs and landings.

### Jedi Wingmen

THE V-19'S SUPERIOR maneuverability a[...]
the best clone pilots to keep up more e[...]
with Jedi starfighters, such as the Delta[...]
interceptor flown by Ahsoka Tano.

# V-19 TORRENT

PROTOTYPES OF THIS heavily armored, maneuverable
fighter first saw combat at the very beginning of the
Clone Wars, flying against Separatist forces in the Battle
of Geonosis. Originally used to protect gunships from
enemy starfighters during planetary assaults, the V-19's
versatility soon won it a place in the fighter
complements of many Jedi cruisers.

### DATA FILE

MANUFACTURER: Slayn & Korpil

MODEL: V-19 Torrent
Starfighter

CLASS: Starfighter

WIDTH: 12.42m (40.67ft)

CREW: 1

WEAPONS: Laser Cannons,
Missile Launchers

AFFILIATION: Republic

# INSIDE THE
# V-19 Torrent

THE V-19 PLAYS a dual role in Republic task forces: Its armor and missile launchers give it enough punch to assault Separatist capital ships or ground targets, while its speed and rapid-fire laser cannons are useful for supporting planetary assaults or dogfighting with enemy fighters. The V-19 lacks shields, relying instead on heavy armor and maneuverability in combat.

*Canopy slides upward here but forward on some models*

*Flight computer*

*Short-range scanners*

*Transceiver/ jammer array*

## Changing Capabilities
The first V-19s needed carriers or hyperdrive rings for supralight travel. Later models added this capability.

*Bow power cells*

*Portside targeting array*

## Target Acquisition
THE V-19'S COMBINATION of wing-tipped laser cannons and missiles proves potent. Unlike assault fighters such as the plodding Y-wing, the Torrent is relatively speedy and maneuverable. Incom engineers replicated this combination of offense and speed for the ARC-170, which replaced many V-19s late in the war.

## Cockpit Controls
The V-19 prototype's cockpit systems were originally conceived for insectoid Verpine pilots. A joystick was added for human pilots and the dashboard was adapted for single-spectrum eyes rather than the keen compound eyes of Verpine.

*Fuel bottles*

*Conductive missile launching strip*

*High-power energy cell*

*Missile*

*Launch tube*

*Reactor heat sinks*

*Reactor*

*Power converters*

*Late-addition hyperdrive*

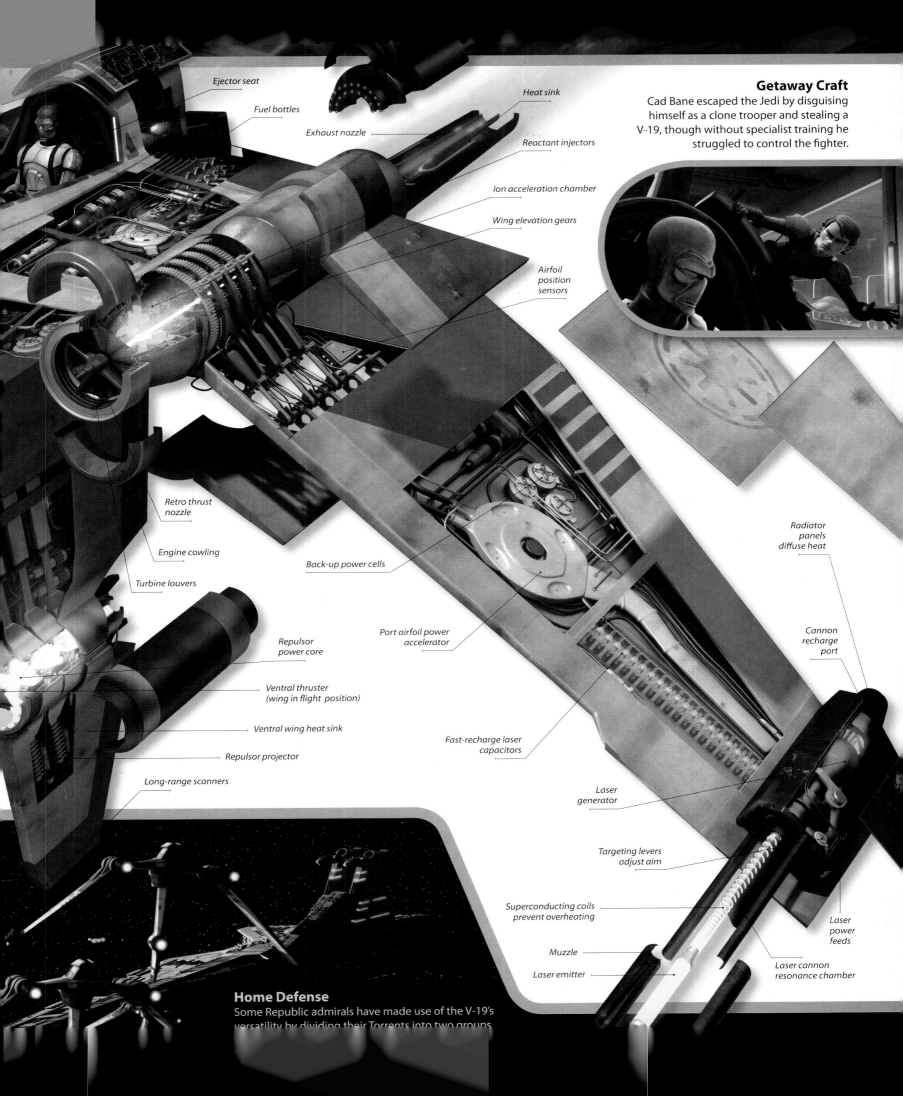

Ejector seat

Fuel bottles

Exhaust nozzle

Heat sink

Reactant injectors

Ion acceleration chamber

Wing elevation gears

Airfoil position sensors

**Getaway Craft**
Cad Bane escaped the Jedi by disguising himself as a clone trooper and stealing a V-19, though without specialist training he struggled to control the fighter.

Retro thrust nozzle

Engine cowling

Turbine louvers

Back-up power cells

Radiator panels diffuse heat

Repulsor power core

Ventral thruster (wing in flight position)

Ventral wing heat sink

Repulsor projector

Port airfoil power accelerator

Cannon recharge port

Long-range scanners

Fast-recharge laser capacitors

Laser generator

Targeting levers adjust aim

Superconducting coils prevent overheating

Laser power feeds

Muzzle

Laser cannon resonance chamber

Laser emitter

**Home Defense**
Some Republic admirals have made use of the V-19's versatility by dividing their Torrents into two groups

# REPUBLIC GROUNDCRAFT

ANCIENT WISDOM HOLDS that the best way to destroy your enemy is at a distance—but sometimes armies must fight on the ground and at close range. The clone troopers who serve the Grand Army of the Republic have a host of vehicles at their disposal for this purpose, from heavy walkers and wheeled tanks to speedy, bird-like recon AT-RTs.

## DATA FILE

MANUFACTURER: Rothana Heavy Engineering

MODEL: AT-TE Assault Walker

CLASS: Walker

LENGTH: 22.02m (72.25ft)

CREW: 7

WEAPONS: Laser Cannons, Projectile Cannon

AFFILIATION: Republic

## AT-TE

WITH SIX STABLE legs, these walkers are able to trudge over uneven terrain and even climb near-vertical slopes. The AT-TE's heavy weaponry and tough armor generally place it at the front of a Republic attack.

*Very responsive controls demand a steady hand*

*Hatch opens downward to become boarding ramp*

*Magnetic feet feature turbo-fired toe grips*

## AT-RT

IDEAL FOR RECON missions, AT-RTs have long speedy legs that can cover a lot of ground quickly and offer their drivers a high vantage point for scanning the area. AT-RT drivers take pride in their skills and this perilous duty.

## DATA FILE

MANUFACTURER: Rothana Heavy Engineering

MODEL: AT-RT Recon Walker

CLASS: Walker

HEIGHT: 3.43m (11.25ft)

CREW: 1

WEAPONS: Laser Cannon

AFFILIATION: Republic

## Stun Tank

DESIGNED TO GROUND enemy warships before they can take flight, the Republic's Stun Tanks were once hastily deployed against a living foe when the Zillo Beast rampaged across Coruscant.

*Ionization chamber is heavily shielded*

*Observation hatch retrofitted with cannon*

### DATA FILE

MANUFACTURER: Rothana Heavy Engineering

MODEL: RX-200 *Falchion*-class Assault Tank

CLASS: Tank

LENGTH: 28.63m (93.92ft)

CREW: 2

WEAPONS: Ion Cannon, Anti-personnel Cannons

AFFILIATION: Republic

### DATA FILE

MANUFACTURER: Kuat Drive Yards

MODEL: HAV wA6 Juggernaut

CLASS: Tank

LENGTH: 28.51m (93.5ft)

CREW: 18

WEAPONS: Laser Cannons, Rocket Grenade Launchers

AFFILIATION: Republic

## Juggernaut

THESE 10-WHEELED war machines can turn tightly and easily cross rough terrain. A cockpit at either end allows them to change direction very quickly.

*Gunner can access targeting information by voice command*

*Barrel can elevate to target enemy aircraft*

## AV-7 Antivehicle Cannon

THESE ARTILLERY UNITS can reposition themselves to allow officers to change attack and defense strategies with ease. AV-7 gunners are held in awe for their bravery, selecting targets while exposed to enemy fire.

### DATA FILE

MANUFACTURER: Taim & Bak

MODEL: AV-7 Antivehicle Cannon

CLASS: Artillery

LENGTH: 15.38m (50.42ft)

CREW: 1

WEAPONS: Laser Cannons

AFFILIATION: Republic

A laser blast from a spider droid leads to a catastrophic loss of power to the portside middle leg engine, destabilizing an AT-TE. A second blast rips it off the cliff face.

AT-TEs use pistons to drive their durasteel "toes" into the rock and electro-grapples to keep hold of the cliff face. But they aren't rated for near-vertical slopes. Anakin is taking a dangerous risk.

Clone sappers use their rifles' ascension cables to make a harrowing climb up the cliff face while laser blasts and projectiles carve out chunks of rock all around them.

# AT-TE:
# ASSAULT ON TETH

The ankle servomotor discs coordinate movement with foot orientation pistons that can be programmed to ram the foot's extended toes into the rock beneath them.

# Uphill Battle

ON A MISSION to find Jabba the Hutt's kidnapped son, Anakin, Ahsoka, and the clone troopers of Torrent Company must scale a towering butte on Teth. The assault won't be easy: AT-TEs are designed to climb steep hills, but here they face a near-vertical ascent under intense fire from Separatist droids atop the mountain.

The gunner manning the AT-TE's heavy projectile cannon must coordinate his fire with the driver: The cannon's recoil could dislodge the AT-TE if fired when the legs aren't firmly seated in the rock.

# HYPERSPACE

HYPERSPACE IS A DIMENSION through which starships can travel faster than the speed of light, allowing them to cross the vast distances between star systems in days or even hours. Without hyperspace travel, the galaxy's civilization wouldn't exist, as planets would be too far apart to communicate. The Republic and Separatists constantly battle for control of the fastest routes through hyperspace.

## Hyperspace Rings

MANY STARFIGHTERS lack internal hyperdrives. To travel through hyperspace, their pilots dock with external hyperdrive rings, which hurl the ship into hyperspace and then wait parked in space until the mission is completed

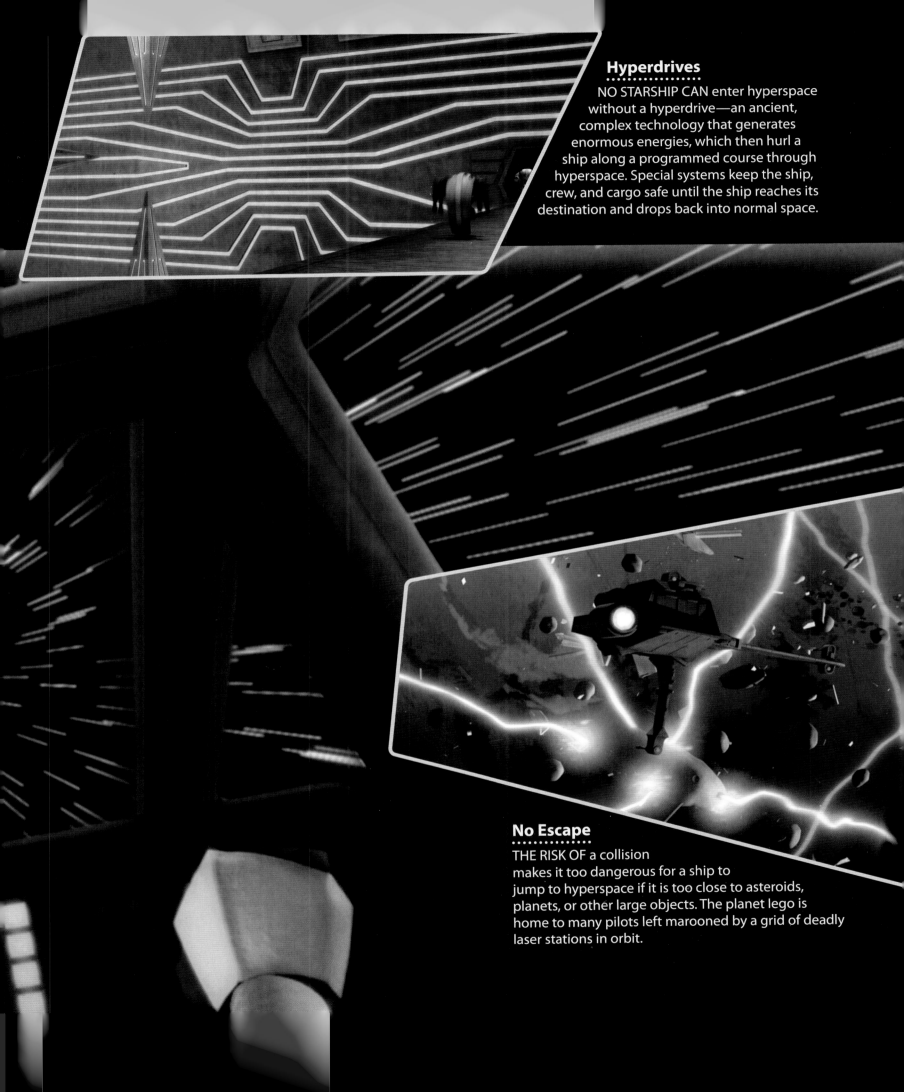

## Hyperdrives

NO STARSHIP CAN enter hyperspace without a hyperdrive—an ancient, complex technology that generates enormous energies, which then hurl a ship along a programmed course through hyperspace. Special systems keep the ship, crew, and cargo safe until the ship reaches its destination and drops back into normal space.

## No Escape

THE RISK OF a collision makes it too dangerous for a ship to jump to hyperspace if it is too close to asteroids, planets, or other large objects. The planet lego is home to many pilots left marooned by a grid of deadly laser stations in orbit.

# PELTA-CLASS FRIGATE

A RELATIVELY NEW addition to the Republic fleet, the *Pelta*-class frigate isn't a front-line warship, but is used in support roles, principally either as a cargo hauler or as a medical craft. Although its tough armor and shields allow it to absorb considerable damage, it still relies primarily on other warships for protection during battle.

Auxiliary wings rotate inward to present smaller profile

## Quick-Change Artist

THE PELTA IS a highly modular craft, and workers can change out its systems and interiors in hours at a shipyard. A Pelta generally carries no weapons while on medical missions.

Starboard airlock leads to main corridor

## DATA FILE

MANUFACTURER: Kuat Drive Yards

MODEL: *Pelta*-class Frigate

CLASS: Frigate

LENGTH: 282.24m (932.5ft)

CREW: 900

WEAPONS: Turbolasers, Point-defense Laser Cannons

AFFILIATION: Republic

# REPUBLIC MEDCENTER

THESE GREAT SPOKED space stations are giant floating hospitals with their own transport systems and power generators. They can treat nearly 80,000 wounded clone troopers in their eight medical bays, offering everything from bacta treatments to prosthetic limbs.

*Pelta frigates dock vertically in bays*

*Main reactor is heavily shielded*

## Wartime Refuge

THE FIRST MEDCENTER, near Kaliida Shoals, was created from a refurbished merchant hub. The Republic then commissioned 19 more such stations—one for each of its Sector Armies.

### DATA FILE

MANUFACTURER: VenteX Construction Yards

MODEL: *Haven*-class Medical Station

CLASS: Space Station

DIAMETER: 651.84m (2,138.5ft)

CREW: 150

WEAPONS: None

AFFILIATION: Republic

# SEPARATIST WARSHIPS

THE MEMBERS of the Confederacy of Independent Systems (CIS) contribute droid armies and warships to the Separatist cause. Many of the capital ships that guard the CIS originally served the greedy megacorporations that encouraged Count Dooku's talk of secession from the Galactic Republic.

## DATA FILE

MANUFACTURER: Hoersch-Kessel Drive Inc.

MODEL: Modified *Lucrehulk*-class LH-3210 Cargo Freighter

CLASS: Star Destroyer

LENGTH: 3,356m (11,014ft)

CREW: 150

WEAPONS: Turbolasers, Laser Cannons

AFFILIATION: Separatists

*Turbolasers rotate inwards when not in operation*

## Lucrehulk Battleship

THESE CRESCENT-SHAPED battleships began as Trade Federation freighters, but the Neimoidians converted them into warships to protect their cargos. Many are now in Separatist service.

## Commerce Guild Destroyer

PRODUCED IN Techno Union shipyards, these warships are the largest ships in the Separatist fleet. A single destroyer is more than a match for the Republic's Venator Star Destroyer.

## DATA FILE

MANUFACTURER: Hoersch-Kessel/Free Dac Volunteers

MODEL: *Recusant*-class Light Destroyer

CLASS: Cruiser

LENGTH: 2,544m (8,345ft)

CREW: 300

WEAPONS: Turbolasers, Laser Cannons

AFFILIATION: Separatists

SEE ALSO

*MALEVOLENCE*
Pages 34–39

## DATA FILE

MANUFACTURER: Hoersch-Kessel/Gwori

MODEL: *Munificent*-class Star Frigate

CLASS: Heavy Cruiser

LENGTH: 1,199m (3,932ft)

CREW: 200

WEAPONS: Turbolasers, Ion Cannons, Point-defense Laser Cannons

AFFILIATION: Separatists

# Banking Clan Frigate

THESE FRIGATES FORM a communications network for the Separatist Navy, and are used to jam Republic warships' sensors, targeting systems, and communications.

**Military Muscle**
Before the Clone Wars, the Banking Clan used its frigates to guard its vaults and to collect on debts owed by planets.

*Control center where droid crew receives orders*

# C-9979 Landing Ship

THE DESIGN OF these giant transports was borrowed from a Trade Federation cargo barge. The new ship is fitted to carry massive droid armies and ground vehicles for assaults on worlds loyal to the Republic.

*Main deployment doors open to reveal access ramp*

## DATA FILE

MANUFACTURER: Haor Chall Engineering

MODEL: C-9979 Landing Craft

CLASS: Gunship

WIDTH: 149.28m (490.75ft)

CREW: 88

WEAPONS: Laser Cannons

AFFILIATION: Separatists

**Death From Below**
C-9979s are vulnerable while descending to planetary surfaces and so rely on their tough armor and vulture droid escorts for protection.

## Supply Lines

THE PLANET CHRISTOPHSIS sits on a crucial trade route at the edge of Outer Rim. The Separatists blockade Christophsis to cut supply lines to several clone armies, but it's not long before a Jedi-led group liberates the planet.

## Navicomputers

TO TRAVEL THROUGH hyperspace, ships' computers must know the location of every star, planet, and moon along the way. If you have the wrong data, you might hit something.

# NAVIGATION

HYPERSPACE CAN BE a dangerous place, so ships follow established, mapped-out trade routes that are known to be safe. Control of these navigation lanes means control in the war, so the Republic and the Separatist forces constantly battle over strategically important planets located on the main routes or at the intersection of key byways.

## Watching the Skies

KAMINO SUPPLIES CLONES for the Republic's armies, and so the trade routes to that planet are monitored carefully from lonely outposts like this one on the Rishi Moon.

## Far From the Front

CAPITAL WORLDS LIKE Coruscant are far behind the front lines of the war, leaving their citizens to pore over star maps to learn how the Republic and Separatist war efforts are faring.

## Secret Routes

Scouts and spies from both sides work to find new navigation routes that would give their military an advantage. The Nexus Route, discovered by Even Piell, is particularly promising.

## What the Hutts Know

THE HUTTS KEEP tight control of their territory and use many secret routes for their illegal activities. Both the Republic and the Separatists seek the Hutts' assistance in the hope of safe passage and secret short-cuts.

## Grievous Command

SUPREME COMMANDER OF the Droid Army, General Grievous took control of the *Malevolence* and quickly began to wreak havoc with it, devastating targets from the Core of the galaxy to the Outer Rim.

FRONT VIEW

## Superweapon

Ion cannons have been a part of starship warfare for many thousands of years, but there is no record of ion weapons as large as the *Malevolence*'s ever having been built. This is evidence that the Separatist shipwrights made a technological breakthrough.

SIDE VIEW

# MALEVOLENCE

A MASSIVE WARSHIP able to disable entire task forces with blasts from its ion pulse cannons, the *Malevolence* was built to instil terror. Count Dooku commissioned the dreadnought because he knew the worlds of the Republic would clamor for protection against it, and the Republic fleets would be forced to waste invaluable time and effort hunting it in the vastness of space.

## DATA FILE

**MANUFACTURER:** Free Dac Volunteers/Pammant Docks

**MODEL:** *Subjugator*-class Heavy Cruiser

**CLASS:** Dreadnought

**LENGTH:** 4,845m (15,896ft)

**CREW:** 900 (Droids)

**WEAPONS:** Ion Pulse Cannons, Turbolasers, Point-defense Laser Cannons

**AFFILIATION:** Separatists

# INSIDE THE
# Malevolence

THE SEPARATIST SCIENTISTS who developed the *Malevolence* managed to make the power generators, capacitors, and feeds for the deadly ion cannons smaller than experts had previously thought possible. But the ship is still one of the largest warships in galactic history, with much of its interior dedicated to powering the cannons and keeping them operational.

## Kinks in the System

THE *MALEVOLENCE* IS something of a flying experiment, as Grievous discovers: Its cannon blasts are barely controllable, and firing often causes energy to bleed back into its other systems, knocking out shields, communications, and engines.

Crew ready rooms

Turbolasers

Partial accelerators maintain stasis field in hyperspace

Laser cannons

Topside crew decks

Forward batteries

Point-defense laser cannons

Maintenance crew levels

Short-range sensors

Tertiary command bridge

Battle droid storage

Docking bays reserved for ground assaults

## Massive Short-Circuit

An ion blast unleashed by the pulse cannon moves at tremendous velocity, catching up with all but the speediest ships and damaging their electrical systems, overloading circuits, and leaving the ships dead in space.

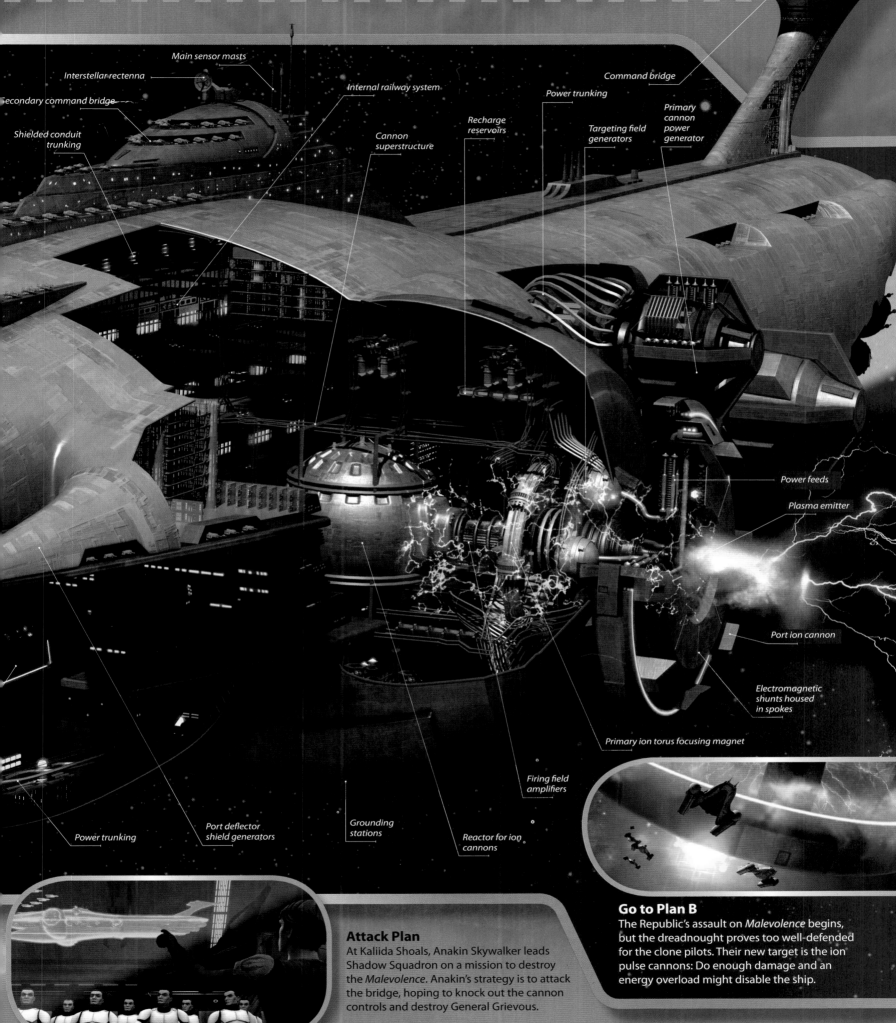

Main sensor masts

Interstellar rectenna

Secondary command bridge

Shielded conduit trunking

Internal railway system

Cannon superstructure

Recharge reservoirs

Power trunking

Targeting field generators

Command bridge

Primary cannon power generator

Power feeds

Plasma emitter

Port ion cannon

Electromagnetic shunts housed in spokes

Primary ion torus focusing magnet

Firing field amplifiers

Grounding stations

Reactor for ion cannons

Power trunking

Port deflector shield generators

## Attack Plan

At Kaliida Shoals, Anakin Skywalker leads Shadow Squadron on a mission to destroy the *Malevolence*. Anakin's strategy is to attack the bridge, hoping to knock out the cannon controls and destroy General Grievous.

## Go to Plan B

The Republic's assault on *Malevolence* begins, but the dreadnought proves too well-defended for the clone pilots. Their new target is the ion pulse cannons: Do enough damage and an energy overload might disable the ship.

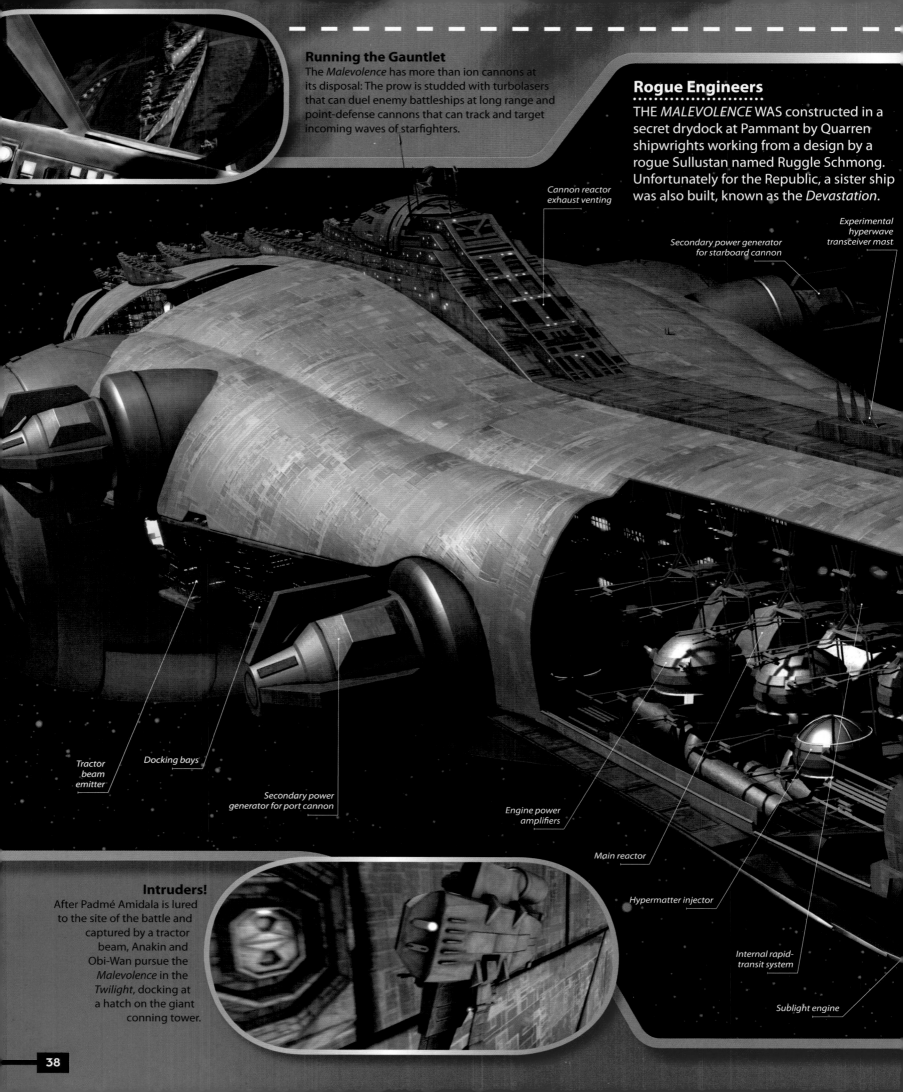

### Running the Gauntlet
The *Malevolence* has more than ion cannons at its disposal: The prow is studded with turbolasers that can duel enemy battleships at long range and point-defense cannons that can track and target incoming waves of starfighters.

### Rogue Engineers
THE *MALEVOLENCE* WAS constructed in a secret drydock at Pammant by Quarren shipwrights working from a design by a rogue Sullustan named Ruggle Schmong. Unfortunately for the Republic, a sister ship was also built, known as the *Devastation*.

Cannon reactor exhaust venting

Secondary power generator for starboard cannon

Experimental hyperwave transceiver mast

Tractor beam emitter

Docking bays

Secondary power generator for port cannon

Engine power amplifiers

Main reactor

Hypermatter injector

Internal rapid-transit system

Sublight engine

### Intruders!
After Padmé Amidala is lured to the site of the battle and captured by a tractor beam, Anakin and Obi-Wan pursue the *Malevolence* in the *Twilight*, docking at a hatch on the giant conning tower.

## Crewed by Clankers
Besides the *Malevolence*'s too-frequent malfunctions, General Grievous is outraged that his crew consists only of dim-witted battle droids. Tactical droids or organic beings would make the ship run much more smoothly.

Point defense cannons

Command bridge

Aft deflector shield generators

Hyperdrive

Thrust nozzle

Supralight engine

Tachyonic discharge prongs

Command crew decks

Turbolift

Emergency airlock

## Hunted
Shadow Squadron's attack overloads both cannons, sending electromagnetic energy surging through the *Malevolence*. Numerous systems are damaged, including the hyperdrive. But the dreadnought remains spaceworthy, and tries to make a getaway.

# SEPARATIST FIGHTERS

THE MEMBERS OF the Separatist movement have contributed many different fighters to the war against the Republic. One of their key strategies is to overwhelm Republic pilots with droid fighters rather than piloted ships.

*Firing channels for energy torpedoes*

## Vulture Droid

PROGRAMMED WITH ONLY basic attack and defense routines, a vulture droid is little match for a living pilot one-on-one. But they make deadly foes when attacking in swarms, ganging up to trap and destroy Republic starfighters.

*Wingtips serve as feet in walking mode*

### DATA FILE

MANUFACTURER: Xi Char Cathedral Factories

MODEL: *Vulture*-class Droid Starfighter

CLASS: Starfighter

LENGTH: 6.96m (22.75ft)

CREW: None (droid brain)

WEAPONS: Laser Cannons, Energy Torpedoes

AFFILIATION: Separatists

### DATA FILE

MANUFACTURER: Baktoid Armor Workshop

MODEL: *Hyena*-class Bomber

CLASS: Starfighter

LENGTH: 12.48m (40.92ft)

CREW: None (droid brain)

WEAPONS: Laser Cannons, Proton Torpedoes, Concussion Missiles, Proton Bombs

AFFILIATION: Separatists

## Hyena Bomber

THE HYENA BOMBER is a refined design of the vulture droid. Whereas vulture droids are designed for dogfights in space, the hyena bomber is adapted to blast cities on Republic worlds into surrender.

*Active-sensor eyes visible through sensor ports*

Bow prongs are typical of Geonosian starship design

# Geonosian Fighter

THE INSECTILE GEONOSIANS fly these speedy, agile craft in defense of their own hives. Efforts to adapt the Geonosian fighter for use by droids or other species have failed, as its flight systems are controlled through scents and pheromones.

## DATA FILE

MANUFACTURER: Huppla Pasa Tisc Shipwrights Collective

MODEL: *Nantex*-class Territorial Defense Starfighter

CLASS: Starfighter

LENGTH: 9.77m (32.08ft)

CREW: 1

WEAPONS: Laser Cannon

AFFILIATION: Geonosian Hives

# Grievous's Fighter

UTAPAU HAS VERY advanced technology, which General Grievous has long coveted for the Separatist arsenal. Although Utapau remains neutral, Grievous has acquired an Utapaun fighter; the *Soulless One*.

## DATA FILE

MANUFACTURER: Feethan Ottraw Scalable Assemblies

MODEL: Belbullab-22 Starfighter

CLASS: Starfighter

LENGTH: 9.68m (31.75ft)

CREW: 1

WEAPONS: Laser Cannons

AFFILIATION: General Grievous

Triple laser cannons offer rapid fire

Forward scanners feed targeting computers

# *Rogue*-class Fighter

SHIPWRIGHTS ON THE neutral planet Utapau built the tough, capable Porax-38 fighter for their world's defense. Separatists captured several P-38s and adapted the design for their own *Rogue*-class starfighter.

Hyperdrive motivator for long-range missions

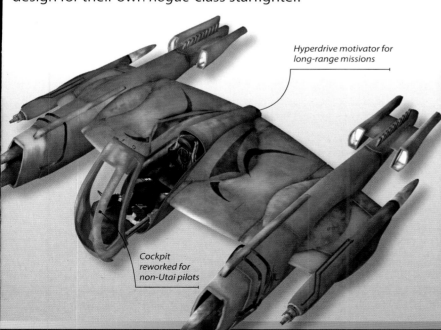

Cockpit reworked for non-Utai pilots

## DATA FILE

MANUFACTURER: Baktoid Armor Workshop

MODEL: *Rogue*-class Starfighter

CLASS: Starfighter

LENGTH: 12.7m (41.7ft)

CREW: 1

WEAPONS: Laser Cannons

AFFILIATION: Separatists

## SEE ALSO

DROCH BOARDING SHIP
Page 43

TRIDENT
Page 47

FANBLADE STARFIGHTER
Page 42

# FANBLADE STARFIGHTER

FANBLADES ARE FAST, maneuverable fighters with retractable solar sails. When unfurled, these sails boost the starfighter's deflector shields and provide an alternative to its sublight engines. Captured Separatist records claim that the Geonosians built six of these fast, maneuverable fighters for Count Dooku, who gave one to his apprentice Asajj Ventress.

## No Hiding

THE HIGH POWER output of its sail makes a Fanblade stand out on the sensors of enemy warships. This is a disadvantage in combat, but Ventress doesn't care: She likes her enemies to know she's coming!

Retractable boom
for solar sail

Portside airscoop
for thrusters

Cannons pivot for use
when sail is furled

Sail membrane increases
deflector-shield strength

### DATA FILE

MANUFACTURER: Huppla Pasa Tisc
Shipwrights Collective

MODEL: *Ginivex*-class Starfighter

CLASS: Starfighter

LENGTH: 13.05m (42.83ft)

CREW: 1

WEAPONS: Laser Cannons

AFFILIATION: Separatists

# DROCH BOARDING SHIP

DROCH SHIPS LOOK harmless enough cruising through space, but dismissing the threat they pose is a mistake. Their four extensible pincers can pierce the hulls of ships, allowing battle droids to board a damaged ship and commandeer it for Separatist use.

*Magnetic grapples lock on to targeted ship*

## Search and Destroy

AS WELL AS boarding large craft, Droch ships can put their metal-piercing skills to use on smaller tasks. After destroying a Republic task force at Abregado, General Grievous sends Droch ships to hunt for escape pods, tear them open, and fatally expose any Republic survivors to the vacuum of space.

*Pincers can pierce durasteel hulls*

## DATA FILE

MANUFACTURER: Colicoid Creation Nest

MODEL: *Droch*-class Boarding Craft

CLASS: Gunship

LENGTH: 18.51m (60.67ft)

CREW: 1

WEAPONS: Laser Cannons, Boarding Drill

AFFILIATION: Separatists

# WEAPONS

DURING THE CLONE WARS, vehicles carry a variety of weapons for eliminating enemy targets. In space, weaponry is needed for everything from attacking starfighters to obliterating ground units on planets below. Both Republic and Separatist scientists are constantly seeking ways of dealing out death and destruction that could tip the balance of the war.

## Turbolasers

TURBOLASERS ARE powerful laser cannons typically mounted on turrets and deployed against warships and planets. They require massive amounts of power, so are only found on large structures like capital ships and orbital platforms.

## Proton Torpedoes

THESE PROJECTILE weapons are fired at high speed from launchers aboard starfighters or capital ships. They can punch through most deflector shields.

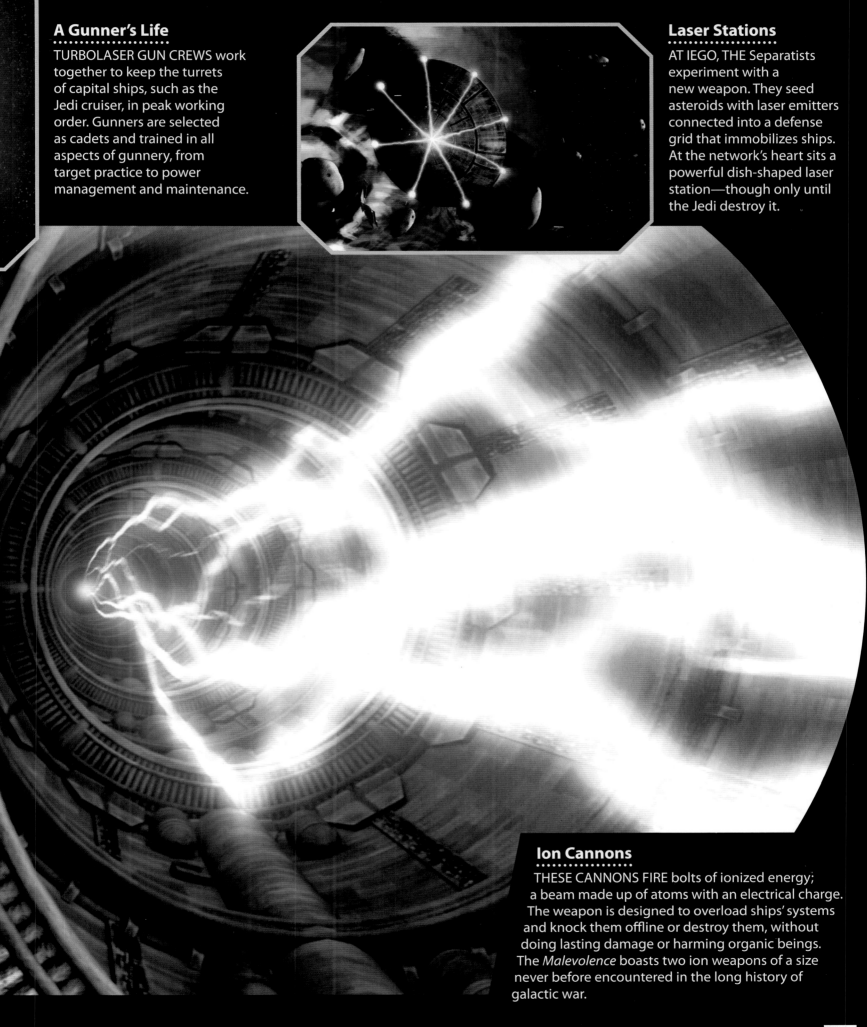

## A Gunner's Life

TURBOLASER GUN CREWS work together to keep the turrets of capital ships, such as the Jedi cruiser, in peak working order. Gunners are selected as cadets and trained in all aspects of gunnery, from target practice to power management and maintenance.

## Laser Stations

AT IEGO, THE Separatists experiment with a new weapon. They seed asteroids with laser emitters connected into a defense grid that immobilizes ships. At the network's heart sits a powerful dish-shaped laser station—though only until the Jedi destroy it.

## Ion Cannons

THESE CANNONS FIRE bolts of ionized energy; a beam made up of atoms with an electrical charge. The weapon is designed to overload ships' systems and knock them offline or destroy them, without doing lasting damage or harming organic beings. The *Malevolence* boasts two ion weapons of a size never before encountered in the long history of galactic war.

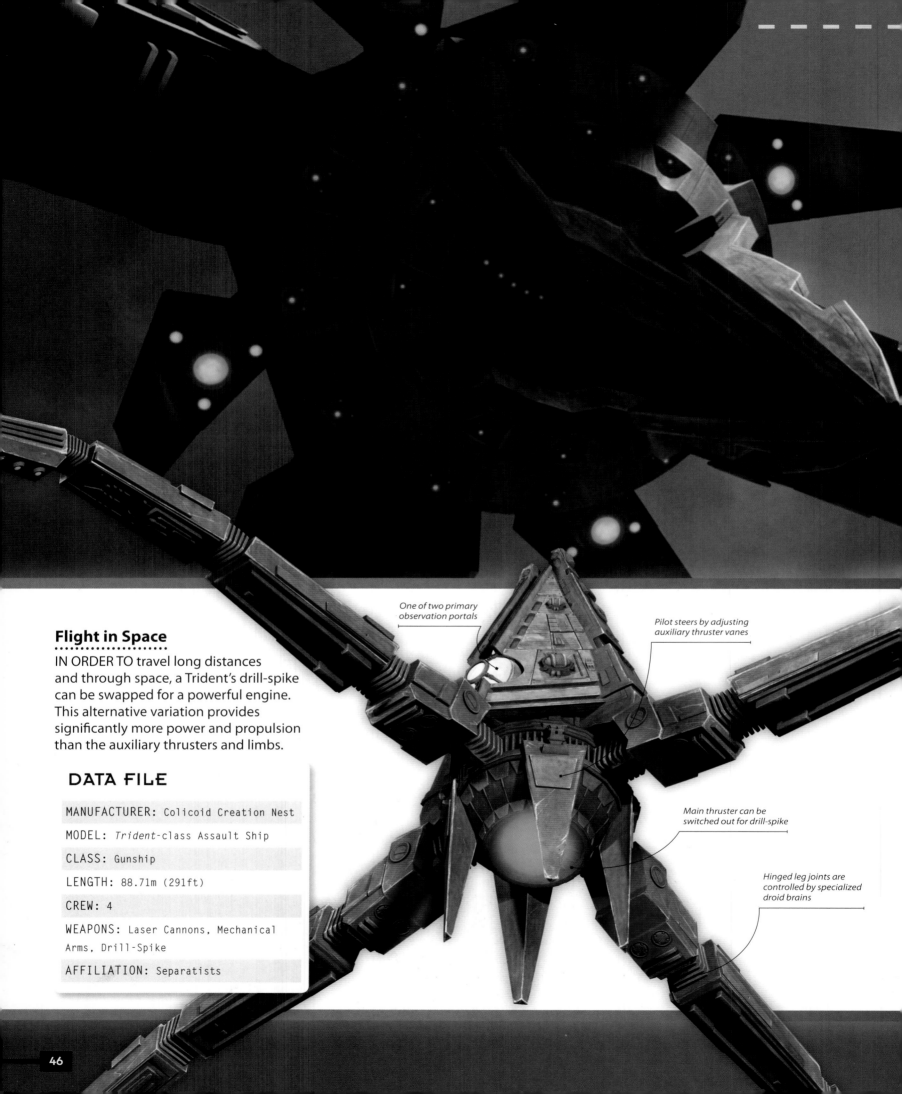

## Flight in Space

IN ORDER TO travel long distances
and through space, a Trident's drill-spike
can be swapped for a powerful engine.
This alternative variation provides
significantly more power and propulsion
than the auxiliary thrusters and limbs.

### DATA FILE

MANUFACTURER: Colicoid Creation Nest

MODEL: *Trident*-class Assault Ship

CLASS: Gunship

LENGTH: 88.71m (291ft)

CREW: 4

WEAPONS: Laser Cannons, Mechanical
Arms, Drill-Spike

AFFILIATION: Separatists

One of two primary
observation portals

Pilot steers by adjusting
auxiliary thruster vanes

Main thruster can be
switched out for drill-spike

Hinged leg joints are
controlled by specialized
droid brains

# TRIDENTS

THE *TRIDENT*-CLASS assault ship is a piloted piece of heavy machinery that draws on an ancient design from the remote Gree Enclave. Thanks to their four whiplike arms, durasteel spike, and laser turrets, Tridents often lead Separatist invasion parties, smashing a path for following battle troops.

### Portable Invasion Force
Tridents are modular, so they can be easily dismantled for clandestine transportation. For example, at Kamino, they are hidden in re-entry capsules and dropped into the sea. Aqua droids who travel inside them then reassemble the Tridents, undetected, on the seabed.

### Shore Leave
Having been reassembled under the Kaminoan sea, Tridents fire their auxiliary thrusters to leap from the waves and reveal themselves. Magnetic grips enable them to clamp onto Tipoca City's outer walls while they ram their drill-spikes home, making way for droid troops to invade.

## Aerodynamic Swimmer

THESE MASSIVE SEPARATIST attack craft can propel themselves through space, air, and water like nightmarish squid. In air and water the aerodynamic machines move as though swimming by whipping their long mechanical legs and using four clusters of auxiliary thrusters for propulsion.

Foot is tipped with magnetic grapples

Thick durasteel armor encases mechanical impeller tendons

Eight pivoting laser turrets protect craft's "head"

One of eight secondary observation portals

A Trident scales a Kaminoan building using its magnetic grapples. The ships' computers have been programmed to seek out a target's optimum locations for drill-spike insertions.

Once a Trident is in the right spot to deploy its drill-spike, it locks all four feet in place and braces its leg impellers against the shock of the spike's impact.

The auxiliary thruster vanes have been rotated up and locked in place to allow the drill-spike clearance to ram through the city's outer wall.

Braced by its quartet of mechanical limbs, the Trident rears back and puts the full weight of its massive head behind a single blow with the drill-spike. Seconds later, the spike is through and droid deployment can begin.

# Ramming Speed

AS WAR RAGES in orbit above Kamino—the principal site of clone-trooper production—a new threat is revealed: Trident ships leap out of the waves, scale the sides of Tipoca City's buildings, and ram their heavy drill-spikes through the walls. Having delivered their aqua droid invaders, the Tridents use their limbs to smash the clone troopers who spring to the city's defense.

# SEPARATIST GROUNDCRAFT

ON THE BATTLEFIELD, the Confederacy of Independent Systems relies on machines to power its seemingly endless armies. Droids are programmed to pilot ground vehicles and other ground units blur the line between vehicle and droid.

## AAT

*Symbol of Confederacy of Independent Systems*

THESE HEAVILY ARMED and heavily armored battle tanks are often commanded by tactical droids, who survey the battlefield from the top turret.

### DATA FILE

MANUFACTURER: Baktoid Armor Workshop

MODEL: Armored Assault Tank

CLASS: Tank

LENGTH: 9.19m (30.17ft)

CREW: 4

WEAPONS: Laser Cannons, Projectile Launchers

AFFILIATION: Separatists

*Main drive tread surrounds central motor*

## Corporate Alliance Tank Droid

THESE SNAIL-LIKE tanks are not very maneuverable, so they attack in lines, blasting away at enemies with their side-mounted weapons.

### DATA FILE

MANUFACTURER: Techno Union

MODEL: NR-N99 *Persuader*-class Droid Enforcer

CLASS: Droid Tank

LENGTH: 10.96m (35.92ft)

CREW: None

WEAPONS: Laser Cannons, Ion Cannons, Projectile Launchers

AFFILIATION: Separatists

### DATA FILE

MANUFACTURER: Techno Union

MODEL: J-1 Semi-Autonomous Proton Cannon

CLASS: Droid Artillery

HEIGHT: 6.46m (21.2ft)

CREW: 1 (optional)

WEAPONS: Proton Cannon

AFFILIATION: Separatists

*Operator's station for manual targeting*

## Proton Cannon

THE POWERFUL SHELLS of a proton cannon are a threat to gunships and transports kilometers above the battlefield. Their legs allow them to shift position, though redeploying them is slow.

## DATA FILE

MANUFACTURER: Techno Union

MODEL: Octuptarra Magna Tri-Droid

CLASS: Artillery Droid

HEIGHT: 14.59m (47.83ft)

CREW: None

WEAPONS: Laser Cannons,
Projectile Launchers

AFFILIATION: Separatists

*Ammunition is stored inside droid's bulbous head*

*Photoreceptors give tri-droid 360 degrees of vision*

# Tri-Droid

A SCALED-UP VERSION of the octuptarra droid, the monstrous tri-droid is a fearsome sight on the battlefields of the Clone Wars, taking aim at distant targets with its laser cannons.

*Tough armor shell retracts to fire warheads*

*Warhead launchers in firing position*

# Super Tank

FIRST DEPLOYED ON Geonosis, the experimental super tank adds more powerful weapons to the tough armor of an MTT, and is intended to defend MTTs and AATs in ground combat.

## SEE ALSO

STAP
Page 76

## DATA FILE

MANUFACTURER: Baktoid Armor Workshop

MODEL: Prototype Super Tank

CLASS: Tank

LENGTH: 12.6m (41.3ft)

CREW: 2

WEAPONS: Laser Cannons,
Warhead Launchers

AFFILIATION: Separatists

*Louvered vents open when armored shell is in place*

*Control room houses battle-droid crew*

## DATA FILE

MANUFACTURER: Baktoid Armor Workshop

MODEL: Multi-Troop Transport

CLASS: Tank

LENGTH: 25.94m (85.08ft)

CREW: 4

WEAPONS: Laser Cannons

AFFILIATION: Separatists

# MTT

THE MTT HOUSES 112 battle droids in an internal rack, ready for speedy deployment and activation. Droid pilots like using its armored nose to smash through walls.

*Armored vents allow waste heat to escape*

# AAT:
# AMBUSH ON RUGOSA

AATs are built with three handholds on each side of the conning tower. Battle droids often ride into battle atop the tank's skirt to keep from wasting their power reserves.

Rather than confront Ventress's troops on open ground, Yoda leads them into the petrified coral forests of Rugosa. He knows that the AATs' primary laser cannons aren't powerful enough to blast a path through the tough coral formations without frequent recharges.

To the frustration of the battle-droid commanders, the coral can't simply be blasted aside by their AATs. Infantry units will have to pursue the Jedi and clones while a route through the forest is found.

# Coral-Moon Contest

IN ORDER TO win the confidence of King Katuunko, an important ally in the war, Yoda agrees that he and his troopers will take on Asajj Ventress's droid soldiers and battle tanks on Rugosa. To defeat the droids and their AATs, Yoda plans to use the moon's petrified coral forests as a defense against the Separatist armor.

The AAT's turret offers an excellent vantage point for battle-droid commanders directing operations. The primary cannon is also fired from here.

Power converters channel energy from the reactor and generators in the tank's rear to forward systems. The converters become very hot during operation, making AATs easy to spot on infrared sensors.

# JEDI STARFIGHTERS

TO SUPPORT THE war effort, Jedi Master Saesee Tiin formed a corps of Jedi starfighter pilots and supervised the creation of the Delta-7B Aethersprite, a new strike fighter built for Jedi reflexes. Jedi Knights' ability with the Force allows them to anticipate events and react with lightning speed. The starfighter's responsive stick and stripped-down systems allow Jedi pilots to fly as fast as they can think.

## Jedi Astromechs

JEDI REPLY ON astromech droids to repair and optimize their starfighters' systems, plot courses through hyperspace, and handle the routine business of spaceflight.

## Restricted: Jedi Only

IN COMBAT A Jedi relies upon the Force for assistance, not technology. Jedi starfighters lack shields, and their armor and sensors are minimal.

Starfighters use hyperdrive rings for faster-than-light travel

Shield projector module

Heat surge radiator

Hyperdrive motivator

Starfighter's shield projector

Previous Delta-7 models had astromech droids set to one side of the cockpit

Viewport polarized against glare from nearby star

Ion thruster nozzle

Link to fighter flight controls

Stasis field generator

Scanning and communications transceiver

Starboard ion drive

## DATA FILE

MANUFACTURER: Kuat Systems Engineering

MODEL: Delta 7B *Aethersprite*-class Light Interceptor

CLASS: Starfighter

LENGTH: 8m (26.2ft)

CREW: 1

WEAPONS: Laser Cannons

AFFILIATION: Jedi Order

### R4-P17
R4-P17 serves as Obi-Wan's astromech. R4 units generally have conical heads, but this one was damaged and rebuilt by Anakin Skywalker using a dome scavenged from an R2 unit.

### R6-H5
A fussy astromech, R6 generally flies with Kit Fisto. He is one of a group of Jedi droids used to test prototype logic modules.

### R3-S6
Nicknamed Goldie, R3 was assigned to Anakin after R2-D2 was lost at Bothawui but R3 had been secretly reprogrammed as a Separatist agent.

### R7-A7
Ahsoka Tano's astromech, R7 is every bit as aggressive and brash as the Padawan he serves—which isn't necessarily the best partnership.

### Clone Wingman
CLONES SUCH AS Axe, Matchstick, and Oddball have trained as pilots throughout their lives, and know how Jedi think and fly in their starfighters. This makes them superb wingmen for the Republic's Jedi aces.

### Jedi Pilots
MOST JEDI ARE capable pilots, but some are truly gifted. They all use the Force to triumph against incredible odds in space battles, but each has their own distinctive style.

### Obi Wan Kenobi
Obi-Wan is an excellent pilot, but detests being behind a fighter's control stick. In his view, flying is best left to droids.

### Anakin Skywalker
Anakin's abilities as a pilot have been legendary since he won a Podrace on Tatooine as a boy. However, sometimes he forgets that his wingmen can't match his skills.

### Plo Koon
The Kel Dor Jedi Plo Koon is a superb pilot known for a strong bond with the clone pilots who fly alongside him in his squadron.

### Saesee Tiin
One of the Jedi Order's best pilots, Saesee Tiin continually seeks to improve the Jedi's fleet of starfighters, pushing new craft to the limits of their capabilities.

### Twin Bridges

A Venator's port bridge handles starfighter flight control, while the starboard bridge serves as the ship's helm.

### A Hive of Activity

With enough crew members to populate a small town, Jedi cruisers constantly hum with activity, whether it's a Jedi general briefing pilots and astromechs about a mission or just the routine tasks required to keep the ship operating.

### Mother Ship

A Jedi cruiser typically carries more than 400 fighters, with its complement including V-19s, ARC-170s, or Eta-2 interceptors depending on the mission. The Venator's long dorsal flight deck allows dozens to launch together.

# JEDI CRUISER

THANKS TO ITS VERSATILITY, the Jedi cruiser is the backbone of the Republic Navy. The warship is capable of serving as a carrier for fighters, bringing heavy guns to bear against other capital ships, or landing on war-torn planets to launch ground assaults.

## DATA FILE

MANUFACTURER: Kuat Drive Yards

MODEL: *Venator*-class Star Destroyer

CLASS: Star Destroyer

LENGTH: 1,155m (3,791.5ft)

CREW: 7,400

WEAPONS: Turbolasers, Proton Torpedoes, Point-Defense Laser Cannons

AFFILIATION: Republic

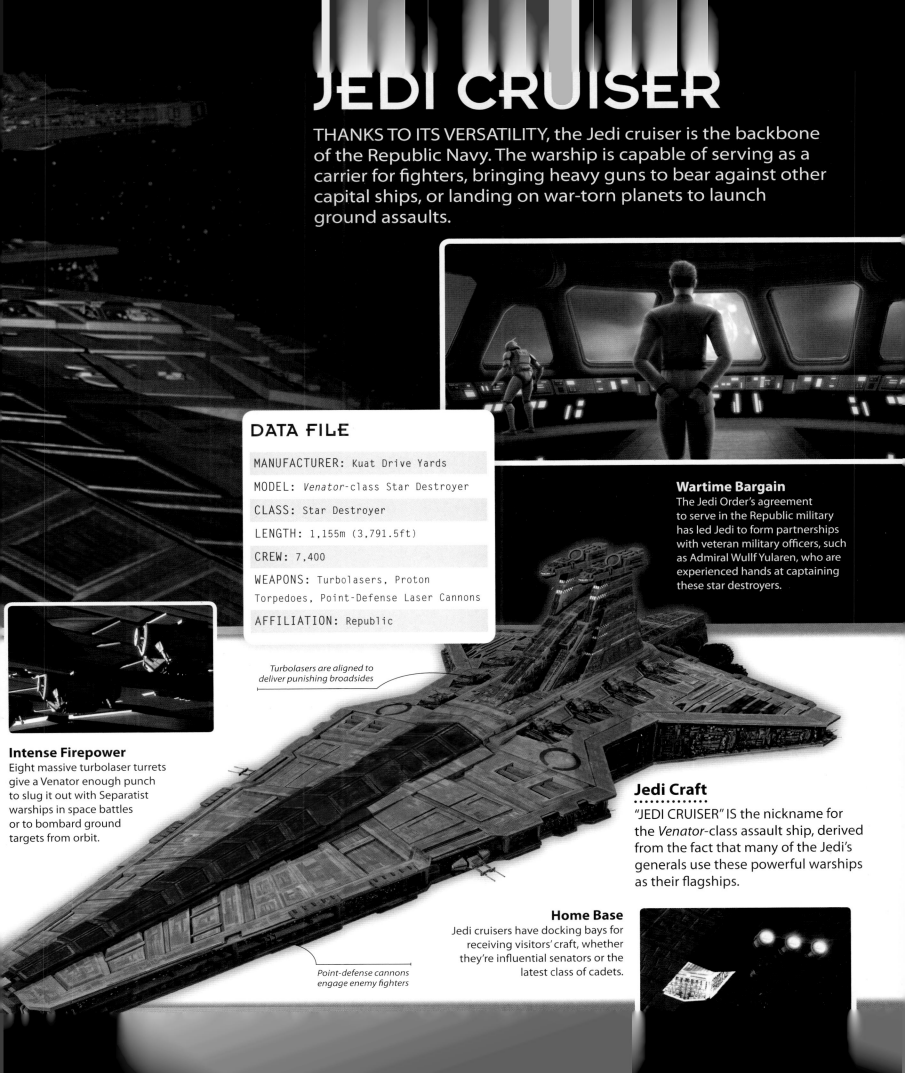

*Turbolasers are aligned to deliver punishing broadsides*

**Intense Firepower**
Eight massive turbolaser turrets give a Venator enough punch to slug it out with Separatist warships in space battles or to bombard ground targets from orbit.

*Point-defense cannons engage enemy fighters*

**Wartime Bargain**
The Jedi Order's agreement to serve in the Republic military has led Jedi to form partnerships with veteran military officers, such as Admiral Wullf Yularen, who are experienced hands at captaining these star destroyers.

**Jedi Craft**
"JEDI CRUISER" IS the nickname for the *Venator*-class assault ship, derived from the fact that many of the Jedi's generals use these powerful warships as their flagships.

**Home Base**
Jedi cruisers have docking bays for receiving visitors' craft, whether they're influential senators or the latest class of cadets.

Admiral Kilian and the handful of officers who stayed aboard the *Endurance* were on the starboard helm-and-command bridge, which remained intact thanks to superb piloting by the cruiser's helmsman.

After Boba Fett sabotaged the *Endurance*'s main reactor, the explosion ripped through the starboard aft quarter of the ship, crippling its engines and making its demise inevitable.

# Crash on Vanqor

AFTER THE CRIPPLED *Venator*-class Star Destroyer, the *Endurance*, plunges into the atmosphere of Vanqor, Anakin Skywalker and Mace Windu follow the trail of destruction to the ship's crash site. The devastation is terrible, but the ship remains right side up with its bridges intact. It's possible that some of its crew may have survived.

R8-B7 is Mace Windu's astromech. He is programmed to be more businesslike than Anakin's droid counterpart, the brash, spunky R2-D2.

Terrain-following sensors and scanners built into the nose of Anakin's fighters present pilot and droid with a continuously updated stream of data about the fiery wreckage below.

Plugged into the droid socket of Anakin's starfighter, R2-D2 keeps ordering new scans of the *Endurance*'s wreckage. Mace's droid R8-B7 might find the data irrelevant, but the crash site bothers R2—he has what humans might call "a bad feeling about this."

## The Basics

ALTHOUGH STARSHIPS are complex machines, they are fairly simple to fly, with a control yoke and pedals for acceleration and braking. With assistance from an onboard autopilot and spaceport computers, most civilian pilots can handle basic spaceflight.

## Trust your Wingman

ROOKIE FIGHTER PILOTS can quickly become overwhelmed in combat, struggling to keep track of dozens of ships. To survive, pilots must learn to work together.

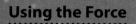

## Using the Force

JEDI KNIGHTS ARE some of the galaxy's best star pilots, thanks to their way with the Force that gives them quick reflexes and the ability to sense danger and see things before they happen. This allows them to anticipate enemy movements and know exactly where to target their weapons.

## Surveying the Battle

THE COMMANDERS OF mighty capital ships leave the flying to helmsmen: Their post is on the bridge—the best vantage point for watching a battle unfold.

# PILOTING

ALL STARSHIPS are capable of flying themselves through hyperspace, and most autopilots can handle everything from takeoff to landing, but piloting for space combat requires more. Organic beings are superior to droids at the required improvisation. And when beings of most species dream of blasting off for the stars, they imagine their own hand—or paw or tentacle—on the starship's control stick.

## Manning the Guns

SOME FIGHTERS HAVE a pilot and a gunner. The best such teams think along with each other, as if they were a single pair of eyes and hands.

## Clone Pilots

THE REPUBLIC'S PILOTS are selected from clones who demonstrate at an early age superior reflexes, vision, strategic thinking, and hand-eye coordination. All have been pilots for most of their accelerated lives.

## Stealth Pilots

THE BEST CLONE pilots may be chosen for secret missions at hidden bases where the Republic tests new warships and fighters. During these tests, as much attention is paid to training as to technology, so new clones can be quickly taught the skills needed to fly new starships.

## Unhappy Landing

AFTER THE *TWILIGHT'S* swing-wing is shot away over Tatooine, Anakin barely manages to land in one piece. The crash severs the starboard laser cannon's powerbus connections, decouples the main battery and short-range sensors, and fills the port airscoop with sand. But as spacers say, sometimes the most important thing about a landing is that you walk away from it.

FRONT SIDE VIEW

REAR VIEW

### Full of Surprises

Old freighters don't come with a manual and their special modifications can surprise new owners. After discovering the *Twilight*'s hidden torpedo launcher, Anakin wonders what else may be hiding beneath the ship's hull plates.

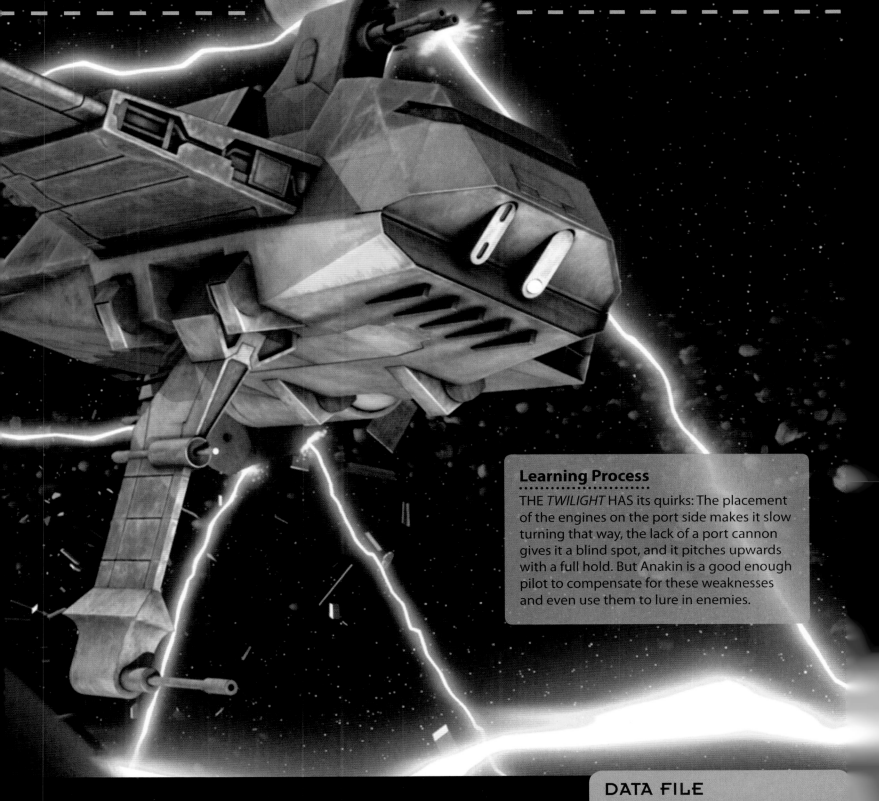

## Learning Process

THE *TWILIGHT* HAS its quirks: The placement of the engines on the port side makes it slow turning that way, the lack of a port cannon gives it a blind spot, and it pitches upwards with a full hold. But Anakin is a good enough pilot to compensate for these weaknesses and even use them to lure in enemies.

# THE *TWILIGHT*

ANAKIN SKYWALKER DIDN'T get behind the controls of the *Twilight* because he liked the battered freighter's looks—it was the only way he and Ahsoka could get off Teth. But having discovered the dingy craft's surprising speed and offensive capabilities, he decides to keep it. A rusty space scow is perfect cover for missions that require discretion. Besides, Anakin is always happiest when tinkering with something mechanical, and the *Twilight* needs plenty of work.

## DATA FILE

MANUFACTURER: Corellian Engineering Corporation

MODEL: G9 Rigger Freighter

CLASS: Freighter

LENGTH: 34.1m (112ft)

CREW: 2 to 4

WEAPONS: Laser Cannons, Torpedo Launcher

AFFILIATION: Anakin Skywalker

# INSIDE THE
# *Twilight*

LIKE MANY OLD freighters, the *Twilight*'s history is murky. One of the first G9 Riggers equipped with a hyperdrive, its swing-wing and armaments were added as a defense against pirates. Ziro the Hutt later bought it and added smuggling compartments for shipments of spice. Anakin Skywalker commandeered the ship and used it throughout the Clone Wars.

## Against Regulations
SOME RIGID REPUBLIC officers object to carrying a dubious ship like the *Twilight* aboard a Navy warship. But while her presence may be against regulations, Anakin makes his own rules: His battered old freighter stays.

*Attitude thrusters*

*Starboard battery*

*Power coupling*

## Pretty on the Inside
Any customs official will tell you not to judge a freighter by its exterior: Spacers love to change out their ships' weapons, shields, sensors, and engines, making modifications that are legal as well as some that aren't.

*Laser focus accelerators*

*Power regulator*

*Drive chain for laser rotary track*

*Short-range sensors*

## Medical Bay
The *Twilight* lacks a medical droid, but does have a hologram of one that checks bioscan results against a medical database.

*Power trunking to laser*

*Lamp*

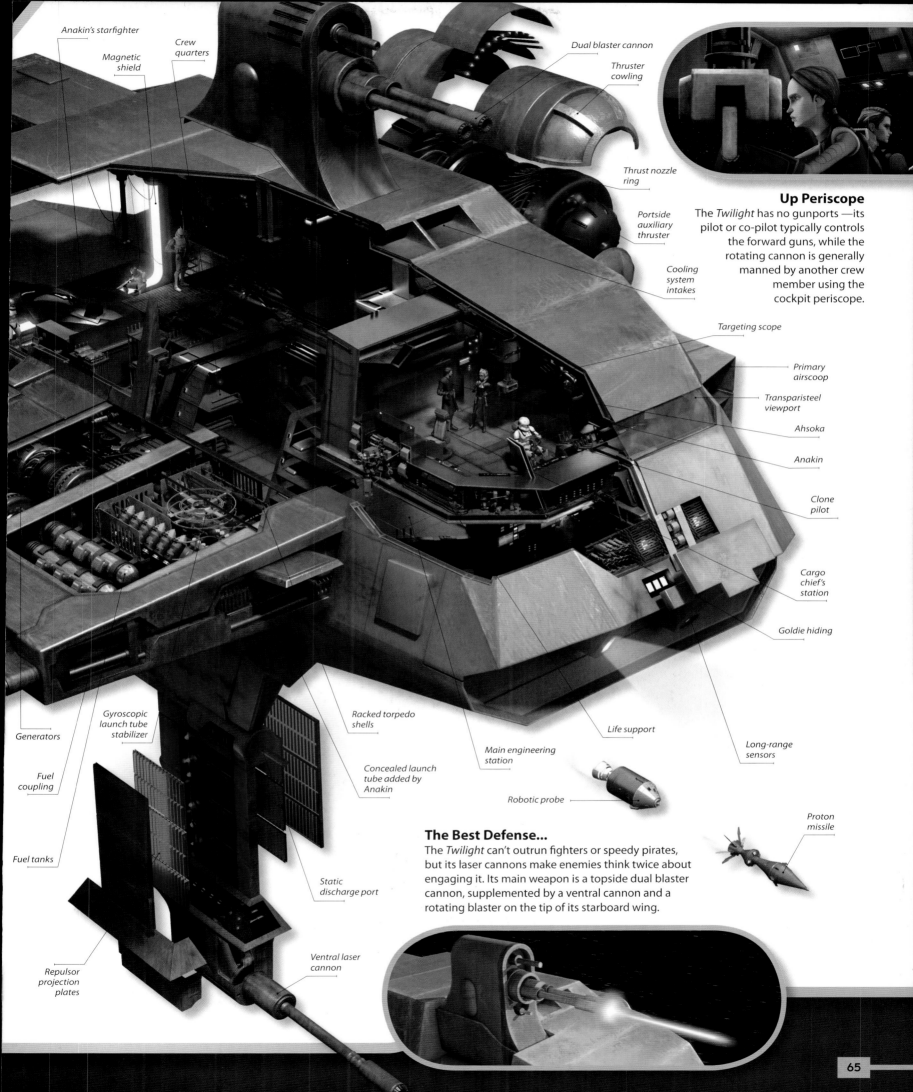

Anakin's starfighter

Magnetic shield

Crew quarters

Dual blaster cannon

Thruster cowling

Thrust nozzle ring

Portside auxiliary thruster

Cooling system intakes

### Up Periscope

The *Twilight* has no gunports —its pilot or co-pilot typically controls the forward guns, while the rotating cannon is generally manned by another crew member using the cockpit periscope.

Targeting scope

Primary airscoop

Transparisteel viewport

Ahsoka

Anakin

Clone pilot

Cargo chief's station

Goldie hiding

Life support

Long-range sensors

Generators

Gyroscopic launch tube stabilizer

Racked torpedo shells

Main engineering station

Robotic probe

Proton missile

Fuel coupling

Concealed launch tube added by Anakin

### The Best Defense...

The *Twilight* can't outrun fighters or speedy pirates, but its laser cannons make enemies think twice about engaging it. Its main weapon is a topside dual blaster cannon, supplemented by a ventral cannon and a rotating blaster on the tip of its starboard wing.

Fuel tanks

Static discharge port

Repulsor projection plates

Ventral laser cannon

*Twin thrusters outperform even police airspeeders*

*Aerodynamic bow aids high-speed maneuvers*

# Jedi Turbo Speeder

OVERSIZED ENGINES AND distinctive axe-shaped fronts make Jedi turbo speeders hard to miss in the Coruscant skies. Fast and agile, they have very responsive controls, optimized for Force-aided reflexes.

**Sensible Flying**
Padawans lent a turbo speeder for Jedi business are routinely warned not to show off while behind the control stick, so as not to offend Coruscant police or the civilians the Jedi have sworn to protect.

## DATA FILE

MANUFACTURER: Slayn & Korpil

MODEL: Praxis Mk. I Turbo Speeder

CLASS: Airspeeder

LENGTH: 12.4m (40.7ft)

CREW: 1

WEAPONS: None

AFFILIATION: Jedi Order

## DATA FILE

MANUFACTURER: Hyrotii Engineering

MODEL: ComfortRide Passenger Airspeeder

CLASS: Airspeeder

LENGTH: 10.55m (34.58ft)

CREW: 1

WEAPONS: None

AFFILIATION: None

# Coruscant Speeder

BUILT-IN NAVIGATION systems help Coruscant's millions of air taxis and speeders find safe routes through the skies. But the system on Duchess Satine's speeder has been sabotaged!

*Mild tractor field helps keep passengers in seats*

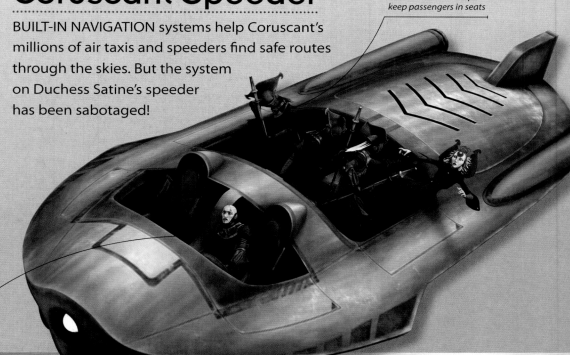

*Aramis struggles to control sabotaged speeder*

# AIRSPEEDERS

AIRSPEEDERS THRONG the skies of many worlds. Most are driven by pilot droids or licensed operators, but on busy worlds, many airspeeders fly themselves, responding to signals from floating navigational buoys.

## DATA FILE

MANUFACTURER: SoroSuub Corporation

MODEL: RGC-16 Airspeeder

CLASS: Airspeeder

LENGTH: 6.26m (20.58ft)

CREW: 1

WEAPONS: None

AFFILIATION: Varies

*Curved housing holds main repulsorlift unit*

# RGC-16

THE RGC-16 IS a typical civilian speeder, similar to millions of models registered to Coruscanti citizens or rented to visitors eager to try their hand behind the stick in the urban world's crowded skies.

*Engine intakes are tipped with variable-beam lamps*

## DATA FILE

MANUFACTURER: Ubrikkian Transports

MODEL: Custom Ubrikkian Speeder

CLASS: Speeder Bike

LENGTH: 5.87m (19.3ft)

CREW: 1

WEAPONS: None

AFFILIATION: Dathomiri Nightsisters

## Nightsister Speeder

THIS ANGULAR CRAFT is difficult to fly, as the pilot must constantly keep the heavy offset turbojet in balance with the lighter sidecar. This suits Dathomir's Nightsisters— for them even piloting a speeder should be a test of will.

**SEE ALSO**

**FREECO BIKE**
Pages 72–75

**JEDI JUMPSPEEDER**
Page 70

**HUTT SWAMP SPEEDER**
Page 71

# NIGHTSISTER SPEEDER: THE TESTING OF SAVAGE OPRESS

Savage Opress has grown up all too aware of the Nightsisters and their periodic visits to claim male warriors as servants, with death awaiting failed candidates. Savage has survived, and now he finds himself a slave of the dark-side women.

Seen through Dathomir's constant veil of fog, the running lights of a Nightsister speeder resemble the eyes of a jungle predator—and the rumble of the engine sounds like the roar of a beast.

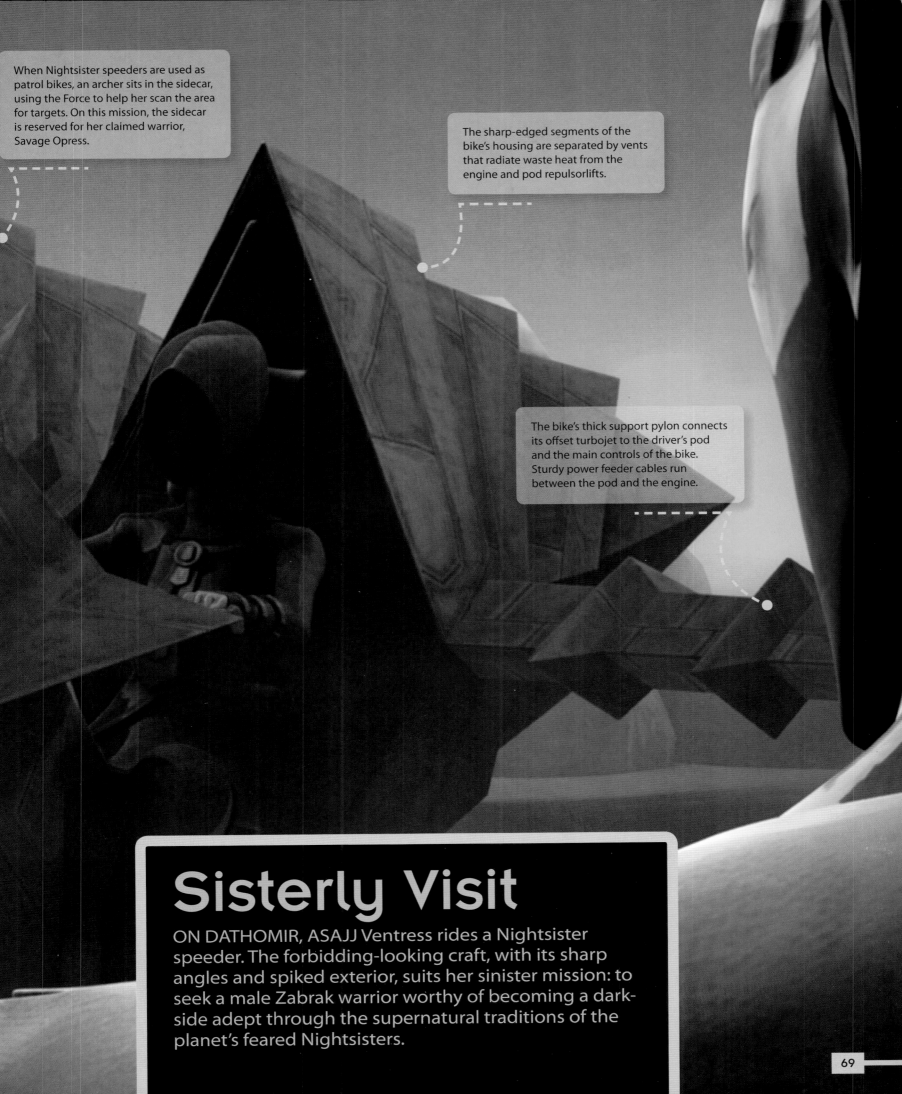

When Nightsister speeders are used as patrol bikes, an archer sits in the sidecar, using the Force to help her scan the area for targets. On this mission, the sidecar is reserved for her claimed warrior, Savage Opress.

The sharp-edged segments of the bike's housing are separated by vents that radiate waste heat from the engine and pod repulsorlifts.

The bike's thick support pylon connects its offset turbojet to the driver's pod and the main controls of the bike. Sturdy power feeder cables run between the pod and the engine.

# Sisterly Visit

ON DATHOMIR, ASAJJ Ventress rides a Nightsister speeder. The forbidding-looking craft, with its sharp angles and spiked exterior, suits her sinister mission: to seek a male Zabrak warrior worthy of becoming a dark-side adept through the supernatural traditions of the planet's feared Nightsisters.

# JEDI JUMPSPEEDER

THE JEDI JUMPSPEEDER is a scooter-style speeder bike originally made for the Jedi Order, but also adopted by civilians. They have proved popular with factory wardens, traffic police, and others whose jobs require them to travel constantly within a limited area. The bikes are not made for speed, as the rider gets no protection from wind during travel.

*Control yoke is adjustable*

## DATA FILE

MANUFACTURER: Kuat Vehicles

MODEL: *Undicur*-class Jumpspeeder

CLASS: Speeder Bike

LENGTH: 1.84m (6ft)

CREW: 1

WEAPONS: None

AFFILIATION: Jedi Order

## A Different Stance

DRIVERS OF THESE repulsorlift scooters typically sit upright, with the bulk of the bike behind them. Variations of the bike that are operated by a driver in a standing position are generally known as "airhooks."

*Operator pylon extends to fit taller riders*

# HUTT SWAMP SPEEDER

THE *PONGEETA*-CLASS swamp speeder is a modern take on the ancient Hutt fanboats; flat-bottomed craft designed to traverse the murky waters of Nal Hutta—a maze of silty channels choked with weeds, downed trees, and other hazards.

## Modern Solution

TO AVOID BECOMING mired in the Nal Hutta, this swamp speeder has a flat bottom. It retains the look of its fanboat predecessor, but has traded old-fashioned propeller fans for high-tech ion cannons and repulsorlifts.

Pressor-field generator pushes obstructions aside

Piloting controls

Pilot's seat elevated for maximum visibility

Auxiliary fan used for maneuvering

### DATA FILE

MANUFACTURER: Ubrikkian Industries

MODEL: *Pongeeta*-class Swamp Speeder

CLASS: Repulsorcraft

LENGTH: 12.31m (40.4ft)

CREW: 1

WEAPONS: None

AFFILIATION: Hutts

## Following Orders

WHEN CAPTAIN REX is ordered to attack Orto Plutonia's Talz using Freeco bikes, the veteran soldier knows his men are risking their lives because of Chi Cho's foolishness. But a lawful order is an order, no matter how ill-advised.

## DATA FILE

**MANUFACTURER:** Bespin Motors
**CLASS:** CK-6 Swoop Bike
**LENGTH:** 5.8m (19ft)
**SPEED:** 440km/h (273 miles/h)
**CREW:** 1
**WEAPONS:** Twin Laser Cannons
**AFFILIATION:** Republic

# FREECO BIKE

THE HARSH CONDITIONS on Orto Plutonia can kill a man within hours, even in insulated armor. With Freeco bikes, patrols can safely and warmly cover kilometers of the icy wastes in search of whatever enemy destroyed the Republic's lonely outpost.

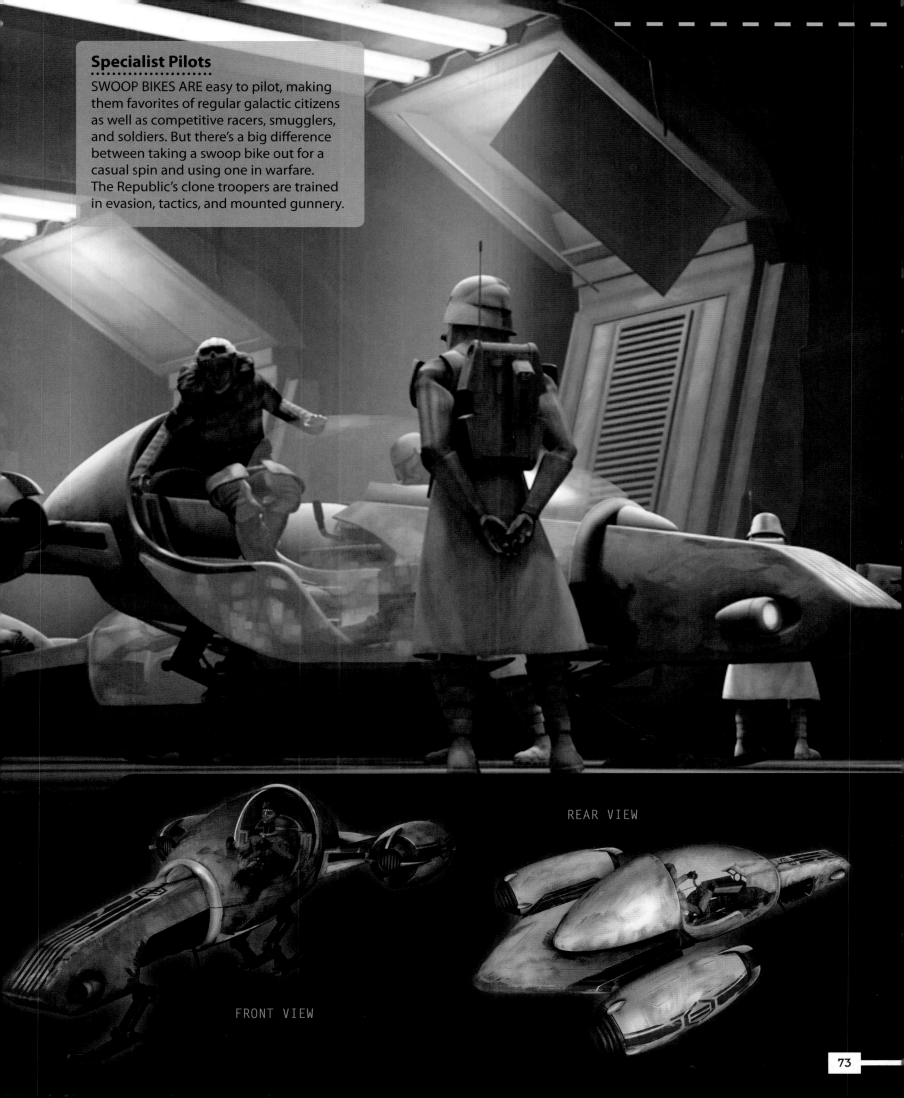

## Specialist Pilots

SWOOP BIKES ARE easy to pilot, making them favorites of regular galactic citizens as well as competitive racers, smugglers, and soldiers. But there's a big difference between taking a swoop bike out for a casual spin and using one in warfare. The Republic's clone troopers are trained in evasion, tactics, and mounted gunnery.

REAR VIEW

FRONT VIEW

## Cho's Folly
Republic troops have been known to ride to war on their Freeco bikes. Pantora's Chairman Chi Cho was convinced that the icy plains of Orto Plutonia belonged to his people and rejected the claim of the primitive Talz to the planet. Under Cho's orders, the piloted CK-6s ventured straight into the frontline.

*Micro-defrost coils keep screen clear*

## Scout Ships
THE FREECO BIKE is primarily intended for use in reconnaissance and scout missions. However, it is also armed with twin laser cannons, designed as antipersonnel weapons.

*Thin duranium alloy skin reduces vehicle's weight*

*Windshield mounting slides along track*

*Radiator cools generator and distributes heat around the bike*

*Collision warning sensors*

*Multi-spectrum headlights*

*Primary sensor array detects heat sources and discerns terrain in whiteout conditions*

*Repulsor core*

*Repulsor projector arms*

*Main subsystem power generator*

## Rocket Ride
BESPIN MOTORS IS a subsidiary of the Incom Corporation, known for speedy, high-altitude swoop bikes such as the JR-4. However, Bespin Motors' CK-6 doesn't have its predecessor's high flight ceiling, as aerial travel is perilous when wintry weather conditions prevail.

*Power converter*

*Non-freezing hydraulic system*

## Specialized Speeder
In freezing conditions, the Freeco bikes are far preferable to the open-cockpit BARC bikes.

*Forward landing skid*

Captain Rex in cold-weather gear

Maintenance panel for wing systems

Heating elements

Atmosphere intake

Laser charge magazine

Thrust unit

Laser cannon and heat sink

### Harsh Conditions

The CK-6's adaptations to the cold range from electrostatic baffles, which keep snow and ice particles out of the engine intakes, to additional insulation and heating elements added to the bike's key systems by Republic engineering teams.

Electrostatic filters keep airscoop clear of ice particles

Stabilizer

Pipe feeds warm air to cockpit

Thrust-vectoring vanes regulate air intake

Additional insulation cobbled together from packing containers

Unit markings pitted by ice impacts

Auxilliary heater

Heating elements

Emergency heat supply

# INSIDE THE
# Freeco Bike

THE CK-6 SWOOP BIKES are designed to shrug off weather that would ground a gunship, allowing troopers to race along just above the snow and ice. No one remembers which Republic jokester gave these "freezing cold" bikes their nickname, but the Republic's troopers found that the name has stuck.

Terrain-following sensor scope

Control yokes with trigger grips

Rear skids

Pressure-activated accelerator pedal

### Behind the Stick

CLONE TROOPERS GIVE the CK-6 high marks for its responsiveness and easy handling, but save special praise for the powerful heating unit built into the acceleration couch.

# SPEEDER BIKES

SPEEDER BIKES ARE used on planets across the galaxy by regular citizens seeking quick transportation. Most models are easy to fly, though impulsive adolescents are warned about going too fast or flying higher than a bike's repulsorlifts can handle. Bikes come in standard models, but garage tinkerers enjoy souping up their components.

## Flitknot Bike

THIS PRODUCT OF the Geonosian hives has been adapted from its original pheromone-controlled systems for use by non-Geonosians. Initially intended for scouting, the bike was unarmed, but a military model now includes a blaster cannon.

*Operator's display scans nearby terrain*

*Twin stabilizer fins ensure steady ride*

### DATA FILE

MANUFACTURER: Huppla Pasa Tisc Shipwrights Collective

MODEL: Flitknot Speeder Bike

CLASS: Speeder Bike

LENGTH: 2.78m (9.08ft)

CREW: 1

WEAPONS: Blaster cannon (strike model only)

AFFILIATION: Varies

### SEE ALSO

PIRATE SPEEDER
Pages 106-107

MANDOLORIAN
SPEEDER BIKE
Page 94

MANDOLORIAN
POLICE SPEEDER
Page 95

## STAP

THE SINGLE TROOPER aerial platform is a stripped-down weapons platform used by battle droids for patrols and recon missions. It evolved from the original design of the civilian "airhook" speeder.

*Pilot controls twin blaster cannons*

*Thruster exhaust is harmless to battle droids*

### DATA FILE

MANUFACTURER: Baktoid Armor Workshop

MODEL: Single Trooper Aerial Platform

CLASS: Speeder Bike

LENGTH: 2.78m (9.08ft)

CREW: 1

WEAPONS: Laser Cannons

AFFILIATION: Separatists

# BARC Speeder

A RUGGED RECONNAISSANCE craft produced for the
Republic military, the BARC was first ridden by elite troopers,
but proved so popular that millions more were ordered.

Driver turns bike by
using control yoke

Paired rear
thrusters help
keep bike stable

Fins stabilize bike but also
divert wind from rider's legs

Blaster
cannons

Airscoop feeds bike's
main turbojet

Captain Rex strapped
to medical travois

## DATA FILE

MANUFACTURER: Aratech Repulsor
Company

MODEL: Biker Advanced Recon
Commando Speeder

CLASS: Speeder Bike

LENGTH: 4.83m (15.83ft)

CREW: 1

WEAPONS: Blaster Cannons

AFFILIATION: Republic

### Military Modifications
Speeder bikes used by law-enforcement
personnel and the military are typically faster than
civilian versions, have more powerful repulsorlifts
that let them fly higher, and have built-in weapons.

# Police BARC Speeder

AFTER THE BARC speeder bike proved popular in the Republic Army,
Aratech was quick to produce a civilian model for police units
patroling the galaxy's many planets.

Coruscant
police droid

Flashing lights
and sirens
are used to
alert civilians

## DATA FILE

MANUFACTURER: Aratech Repulsor
Company

MODEL: RapidRespond Police Speeder

CLASS: Speeder Bike

LENGTH: 4.83m (15.83ft)

CREW: 1

WEAPONS: Blaster Cannons

AFFILIATION: Varies

# Moogan Gunship

MOOGAN GUNSHIPS CAN smuggle cargo in their belly holds, which can be unloaded quickly even in primitive spaceports. On land, these ungainly gunships move around clumsily on their segmented legs—often to scuttle away from authorities.

Cockpit doubles as vantage point for supervising cargo

## DATA FILE

MANUFACTURER: Techno Union

MODEL: *Shekelesh*-class Freight Gunship

CLASS: Freighter

HEIGHT: 21.15m (69.4ft)

CREW: 8

WEAPONS: Laser Cannons

AFFILIATION: Moogans

# Hondo's Frigate

HONDO OHNAKA'S STOLEN flagship is the armed frigate *Acushnet*, one of a class of warships that fell out of favor with Separatist leaders as it wasn't suitable as a droid ship. They were dumped on the used starship market by its disappointed manufacturer, where they became a popular collectors' item.

Docking bay on ventral surface

**An Eye for Starships**
Hondo has a keen eye for ships, and appreciates that the *Corona* class is a knock off of an old and very rare design, the Surronian cruiser.

## DATA FILE

MANUFACTURER: Haor Chall Engineering

MODEL: *Corona*-class Armed Frigate

CLASS: Frigate

LENGTH: 376m (1234.54ft)

CREW: 64

WEAPONS: Turbolasers, Ion Cannons, Point-Defense Laser Cannons

AFFILIATION: Varies

# UNDERWORLD CRAFT

WHILE PIRATES AND crimelords make use of any vehicle they can get their hands on, some craft have become infamous for their popularity with noted criminals—making them even more desired in such circles.

## DATA FILE

MANUFACTURER: Ubrikkian Industries

MODEL: Luxury Sail Barge

CLASS: Sail Barge

LENGTH: 26.28m (86.17ft)

CREW: 26

WEAPONS: None

AFFILIATION: Varies

*Sails principally serve as awnings*

*Steering vanes help guide barge*

## Jabba's Sail Barge

AN OPPULENT PLEASURE craft, Jabba the Hutt's sail barge, the *Khetanna*, floats above the desert wastes and sand dunes of Tatooine on powerful repulsorlifts.

*Decorative plating covers lightweight hull*

*Exposed platform gives 360-degree view for security*

*Controls manned by helmsman*

### Sand Skiff

Jabba's barge is outfitted with blaster cannons, but it always travels accompanied by two sand skiffs. These are faster, more maneuverable craft loaded with armed guards to protect their master.

*Skiffs transport passengers to and from the sail barge*

# HAVE SHIP, WILL TRAVEL

THE TRADE ROUTES of the galaxy and the skies of its worlds are filled with starships of all shapes and sizes. With millions of civilizations in the galaxy, even veteran spaceport workers routinely spot ships that are new to them.

Windscreen mounting slides along track

Thin duranium alloy ski reduces vehicle's weight

## The *Falfa*

THE *FALFA* IS a Pantoran cruiser and the personal sloop of Baron Papanoida. He purchased it second-hand in his earliest days in the Wroonian holodrama industry and has lovingly refurbished it.

**Personal Sloop**
Baron Papanoida uses the *Falfa* as his base of operations, keeping tabs on his far-flung business activities and information network from a luxurious cabin-turned-office.

## DATA FILE

MANUFACTURER: Kuat Systems Engineering

MODEL: *Rainhawk*-class Transport

CLASS: Transport

LENGTH: 20.46m (67.1ft)

CREW: 2

WEAPONS: Laser Cannons

AFFILIATION: Baron Papanoida

**Solid Footing**
In its flying configuration, the *Falfa* has a narrow base, so it deploys three landing skids for better support on land. The sloop's repulsorlift units also kick in when needed to keep the ship balanced.

# Shelter Speeder

SHELTER SPEEDERS ARE mobile laboratories with high-tech sensors that enable scientists to sample air, water, and soil for toxins, radiation, or other threats. The speeder can be sealed to safeguard passengers from exposure to dangerous elements.

*Dorsal bubble gives driver ideal field of view*

**Trouble on Naboo**
Padmé Amidala and Jar Jar Binks use a Shelter Speeder on Naboo to hunt for the source of a mysterious disease killing the planet's livestock.

## DATA FILE

MANUFACTURER: SoroSuub Corporation

MODEL: S-130 Shelter Speeder

CLASS: Airspeeder

LENGTH: 27m (88.6ft)

CREW: 2

WEAPONS: Laser Cannons (optional)

AFFILIATION: Varies

*Toxicity sensor mounts adapted for laser cannons*

**SEE ALSO**

SOLAR SAILER
Page 84

SLAVE I
Pages 85–86

*Ornamental fin houses ship's shield generators*

## DATA FILE

MANUFACTURER: SoroSuub Corporation

MODEL: *Peregrine*-class Star Yacht

CLASS: Transport

LENGTH: 30.59m (100.4ft)

CREW: 1

WEAPONS: Laser Cannons

AFFILIATION: King Katuunko

*Flip-out laser cannons are controlled by pilot*

# Thief's Eye

THIS LUXURIOUS STAR yacht is fit for a king—Toydaria's King Katuunko. It radiates wealth and exclusivity, from its gold and sapphire finish to its streamlined hull. Inside, the cabins are stylishly finished in greelwood and Apokan silveroak.

*Long landing skids keep the curious at a distance*

The *Falfa*'s skirt houses many of her critical systems: repulsorlifts, a suite of short- and long-range sensors, and the communications rectenna Papanoida uses to keep tabs on his galaxywide network of informants.

# Kidnap!

WHEN HIS DAUGHTERS are kidnapped, Baron Papanoida and his son, Ion, take matters into their own hands, racing across the galaxy to the Outer Rim desert world of Tatooine in their Pantoran cruiser, the *Falfa*. Papanoida seeks a meeting with the gangster Jabba the Hutt—and the safe return of his children.

The cruiser's running lights can be swapped out for laser cannons that are controlled from the cockpit.

The *Falfa*'s aft wings are purely decorative. Later Kuat Systems ships with long trunks eliminated them as an unnecessary excess.

The *Falfa* is not particularly fast, but its twin thrusters allow it to make the journey from Jabba's palace in the Dune Sea to the lawless spaceport of Mos Eisley in relatively short time.

# SOLAR SAILER

COUNT DOOKU RECEIVED this sloop as a gift from the Geonosians, but he then asked them to modify it to include a solar sail made of exotic material from an ancient star system. The Separatist leader uses this personal sloop not only for transportation, but as a retreat for his dark-side meditations.

## Space Sailing

DOOKU'S SLOOP NORMALLY relies on its thrusters for propulsion, but in deep space the Count unveils his craft's solar sail, which is more than 100 meters wide. The sail captures energy and harnesses it to pull the sloop along through hyperspace.

FA-4 pilot droid guiding sloop

Prongs are studded with tractor/repulsor emitters

Ship is typical of Geonosian design

## DATA FILE

MANUFACTURER: Huppla Pasa Tisc Shipwrights Collective

MODEL: *Punworcca 116*-class Interstellar Sloop

CLASS: Transport

LENGTH: 14.38m (47.17ft)

CREW: 1

WEAPONS: Tractor/Repulsor Beams

# SLAVE I

*SLAVE I* BEGAN its existence as a short-range patrol craft, but Jango Fett altered it to support his longer-term bounty-hunting operations. The ship has since been inherited by Jango's son, Boba, who continues to upgrade the ship to help him live up to his father's legacy as a ruthless bounty hunter.

## DATA FILE

MANUFACTURER: Kuat Systems Engineering

MODEL: *Firespray*-class Patrol Craft

CLASS: Gunship

LENGTH: 29.15m (95.75ft)

CREW: 1

WEAPONS: Laser Cannons, Seismic Mines, Torpedo Launchers

AFFILIATION: Boba Fett

Cockpit capsule rotates for landings

Vertical altitude requires particular piloting skills

Rotating wings contain powerful repulsorlifts

Twin blaster cannons for short-range use

## More Than Meets the Eye

IN ORDER TO make *Slave I* faster, tougher, and deadlier in a fight, its engines have been beefed up and it is equipped with gear for tracking and disabling enemy targets. Most of the weaponry is concealed to give a false sense of security to potential quarry.

# The Hunter

AFTER THE JEDI cruiser the *Endurance* crashes on Vanqor, Mace Windu's starfighter streaks for the sky. On its tail comes *Slave I*, with Boba Fett manning the guns and Bossk at the controls. Boba has sworn to kill Mace and so avenge his father Jango's death. But can *Slave I* catch the Jedi starfighter?

SLAVE I:
PURSUIT ON VANQOR

Inside *Slave I*'s cockpit, Bossk flies while Boba Fett mans the guns. Urging Boba on is his mentor, the grim hunter Aurra Sing.

*Slave I* flies vertically to offer its pilot better visibility and its gunner a larger field of fire. It takes off and lands "on its back," with the cockpit capsule rotating to keep its occupants sitting upright.

Most astromechs are only programmed for basic maneuvers in a starfighter, but R2-D2 has years of additional programming and data to draw from, thanks to Anakin's refusal to subject the droid to periodic memory wipes. R2 proves a very capable pilot, juking and weaving away from Boba's shots.

The bounty hunters are correct that they are chasing Mace Windu's Delta-7B interceptor, but they don't know that Mace isn't aboard: R2-D2 is flying the fighter by himself.

## Scavenging Arms

THE FOUR GRASPER-ARMS of the *Vulture's Claw* are never still, even when visitors pay a call on Nachkt. The arms are equipped with simple droid brains that identify bits of wreckage and bring promising items aboard for a closer look.

## DATA FILE

**MANUFACTURER:** Gallofree Yards

**MODEL:** GS-100 Salvage Ship

**CLASS:** Freighter

**LENGTH:** 174.78m (573.4ft)

**CREW:** Normally 3

**WEAPONS:** Laser Cannons

**AFFILIATION:** Gha Nachkt

# VULTURE'S CLAW

THE TRANDOSHAN SCAVENGER Gha Nachkt prowls the battlefields of the Clone Wars in this battered, rusty scow, searching for starship components, droids or anything else that he can bring aboard. The ship's holds bulge with salvaged junk he hopes to repair and turn over to the Separatists or the Republic for a profit.

## The Speed of Credits

THE *VULTURE'S CLAW* is much faster than it looks. Nachkt has augmented its supralight engines so that he can beat his fellow scavengers to the site of a battle and get first pick of the wreckage. After capturing R2-D2, he races to Ruusan's Skytop Station in hopes of a reward.

### Tough Hide

Nachkt's ship has military-grade shields and thick armor—features designed not for the rigors of combat, but as a guard against the ever-present danger of collisions in a debris field. For other threats, Nachkt relies on dual laser cannons mounted astern.

FRONT VIEW

### Who's Calling?
Spacers seeking a bargain on starship parts or droids often call on battlefield scavengers, who are happy to unload items that might get them into trouble with the authorities. Eager to do a deal, Nachkt meets Anakin and Ahsoka in the *Claw*'s smelly docking vestibule.

Fuel siphon lines

Salvaged security droid

Salvage sorting area

Communications mast

Fuel reprocessing tank

Massive couplings

Crew quarters converted to storage

Multi-wavelength superscanner

Primary airscrubber

Reactor for superscanner

Multispectrum lamp

Gha Nachkt's quarters

Cockpit

Ventral docking hatch

Inner hatch

Main hold

Turbolift

Terrain-following sensors

Gha Nachkt

Bed

Sensor array searches for chemical signatures of valuable salvage

R2-D2 hidden in cargo compartment

### Scavenger's Secrets
Most of Nachkt's finds sit in the *Claw*'s holds awaiting a buyer, but truly valuable items are squirreled away in hidey-holes throughout the ship.

### Droid Surgeon
Nachkt repairs damaged droids with his vast collection of spare parts. He can also bypass security programs to retrieve information from their memory banks—sometimes the most valuable part.

Dual laser cannons

Elevation pivot

Power trunk

Turret rotation collar

Coolant feed lines

Capacitor array

Steam-heating array

Reclaimed durasteel forged into slugs

Ion acceleration chamber

Attachment point for Gallofree Z-A1 Star Tug

Droid-controlled graspers

Molten processing

Scavenged sensor masts

Smelter

Thrust vector flanges

Aft deflector shield projectors

Hyperdrive generators

Thruster particle stream channels

Mobile smelter

Centrifuge separates valuable materials from slag

Aft power generators

"Elbow" joint

"Wrist" joint

Salvaged escape pod

Work bay gantry

Rotational collar for grasper

Dangerous salvage held in lower hold until it can be decontaminated

### Appalling Conditions
GHA NACHKT'S SHIP is a maze of dingy holds, workrooms, and storage areas. The stale air reeks of burned-out electronics, rancid lubricants, and unwashed Trandoshan.

# INSIDE THE
# *Vulture's Claw*

THIS BEAT-UP OLD salvage ship is perfect for a scavenger like the Trandoshan Gha Nachkt. Huge mechanical claws sift the debris of space, grabbing anything that could be saleworthy. Onboard there is plenty of room for bits and pieces of droids, starships, and who knows what else.

### Treasure Hunt
The *Claw* has a suite of exquisitely sensitive sensors for detecting alloys and chemical traces associated with valuable war matériel. Nachkt also uses simpler detection methods, like a powerful multispectrum spotlight.

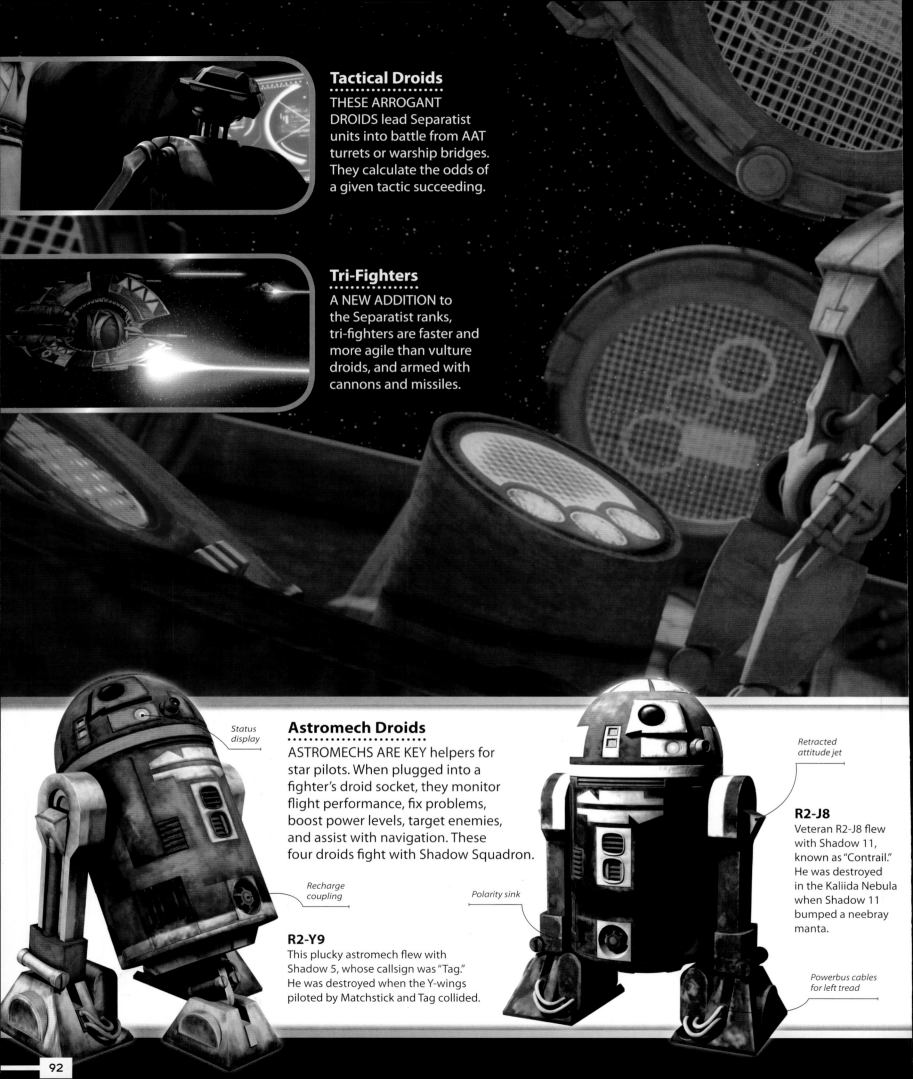

## Tactical Droids

THESE ARROGANT DROIDS lead Separatist units into battle from AAT turrets or warship bridges. They calculate the odds of a given tactic succeeding.

## Tri-Fighters

A NEW ADDITION to the Separatist ranks, tri-fighters are faster and more agile than vulture droids, and armed with cannons and missiles.

## Astromech Droids

ASTROMECHS ARE KEY helpers for star pilots. When plugged into a fighter's droid socket, they monitor flight performance, fix problems, boost power levels, target enemies, and assist with navigation. These four droids fight with Shadow Squadron.

*Status display*

*Recharge coupling*

### R2-Y9

This plucky astromech flew with Shadow 5, whose callsign was "Tag." He was destroyed when the Y-wings piloted by Matchstick and Tag collided.

*Retracted attitude jet*

*Polarity sink*

### R2-J8

Veteran R2-J8 flew with Shadow 11, known as "Contrail." He was destroyed in the Kaliida Nebula when Shadow 11 bumped a neebray manta.

*Powerbus cables for left tread*

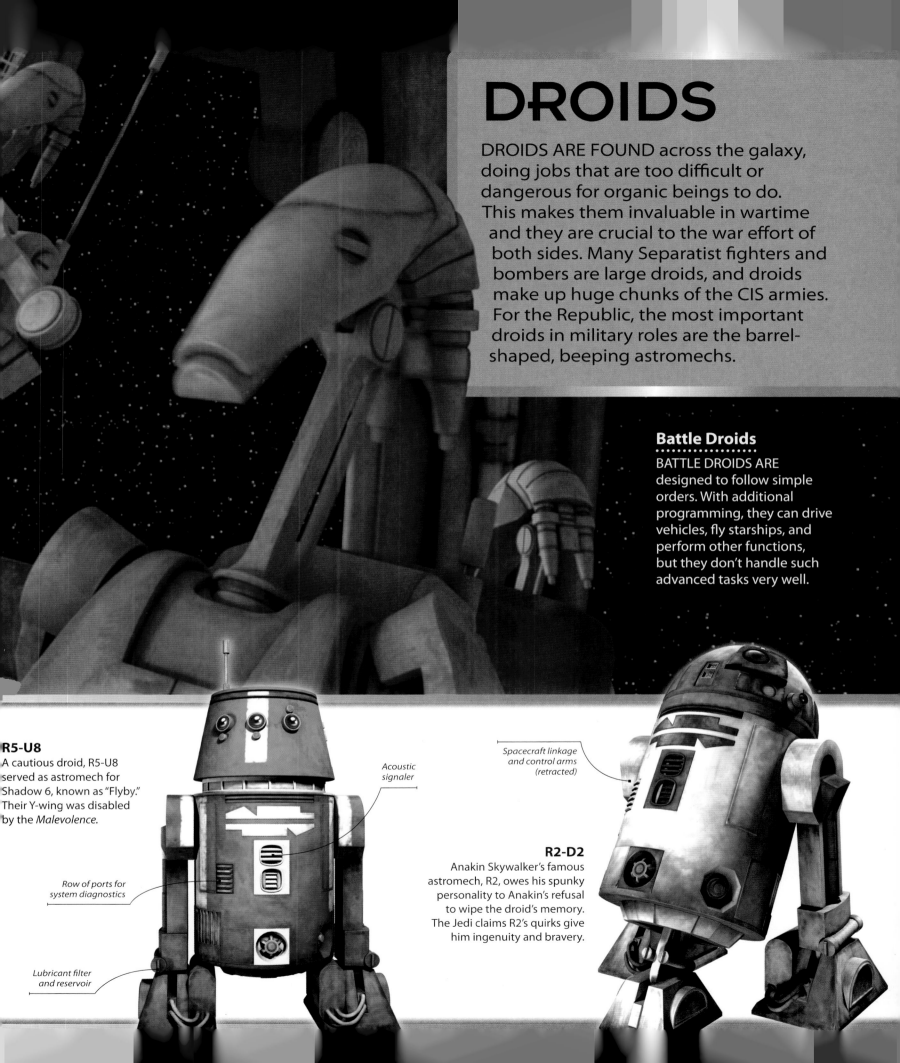

# DROIDS

DROIDS ARE FOUND across the galaxy, doing jobs that are too difficult or dangerous for organic beings to do. This makes them invaluable in wartime and they are crucial to the war effort of both sides. Many Separatist fighters and bombers are large droids, and droids make up huge chunks of the CIS armies. For the Republic, the most important droids in military roles are the barrel-shaped, beeping astromechs.

## Battle Droids
BATTLE DROIDS ARE designed to follow simple orders. With additional programming, they can drive vehicles, fly starships, and perform other functions, but they don't handle such advanced tasks very well.

**R5-U8**
A cautious droid, R5-U8 served as astromech for Shadow 6, known as "Flyby." Their Y-wing was disabled by the *Malevolence*.

*Acoustic signaler*

*Row of ports for system diagnostics*

*Lubricant filter and reservoir*

*Spacecraft linkage and control arms (retracted)*

**R2-D2**
Anakin Skywalker's famous astromech, R2, owes his spunky personality to Anakin's refusal to wipe the droid's memory. The Jedi claims R2's quirks give him ingenuity and bravery.

## SEE ALSO

THE *CORONET*
Pages 96-99

*Wings rotate upward for landing configuration*

*Rear lift handles both passengers and cargo*

# Mandalorian Shuttle

MANDALMOTORS HAS FOUND many buyers for this speedy, swing-wing shuttle, praised for its smooth acceleration and efficient engines. Despite the official line that Mandalorians are peaceful, some customers have armed their shuttles to create an assault craft.

## DATA FILE

MANUFACTURER: MandalMotors

MODEL: *Aka'jor*-class Shuttle

CLASS: Shuttle

LENGTH: 17.97m (59ft)

CREW: 2

WEAPONS: None

AFFILIATION: Varies

## DATA FILE

MANUFACTURER: MandalMotors

MODEL: *Balutar*-class Swoop

CLASS: Speeder Bike

LENGTH: 2.66m (8.7ft)

CREW: 1

WEAPONS: None

AFFILIATION: Mandalorians

# Mandalorian Swoop

A COMPACT SWOOP with a surprisingly powerful engine, the Balutar speeder bike (or "jairgota" in Mando'a) is easy to control even for novice riders because its center of gravity sits below the driver. Patrol models carry twin cannons.

*Power generator sits above main airscoop*

**Obi-Wan's Quest**
A borrowed Mandalorian swoop is ideally suited to Obi-Wan's expedition to investigate mysterious Mandalorian warriors on Concordia, a moon of Mandalore.

# MANDALORIAN SHIPS

DESPITE HAVING BEEN defeated by the Republic centuries ago, Mandalore has retained a distinctive culture and style of technology. In contrast to its proud, warrior past, Mandalore's current rulers espouse pacifism, so their official craft are unarmed.

## DATA FILE

MANUFACTURER: MandalMotors

MODEL: *Kom'rk*-class Fighter/ Transport

CLASS: Transport

LENGTH: 68.1m (223.4ft)

CREW: 4

WEAPONS: Laser Cannons

AFFILIATION: Death Watch

Turbojets designed for rapid startup

## Kom'rk Fighter

ROGUE ELEMENTS WITHIN MandalMotors built these armed transports for the warrior cult known as the Death Watch. Their small size and maneuverability make them capable attack craft.

## Mando Police Speeder

MANDALORE'S POLICE PATROL the skylanes of their planet's domed cities in these airspeeders, relying on their powerful engines to race to crime scenes and respond to emergencies.

Flashing lights are standard on law-enforcement vehicles

## DATA FILE

MANUFACTURER: MandalMotors

MODEL: *Buirk'alor*-class Airspeeder

CLASS: Airspeeder

LENGTH: 10.19m (33.42ft)

CREW: 1

WEAPONS: None

AFFILIATION: Mandalorians

# THE *CORONET*

A LUXURY LINER like those that traveled the spacelanes in a more civilized age, the *Coronet* is a one-of-a-kind model, built by Kalevala Spaceworks as a showcase for Mandalorian engineering, and proof that the planet has left its violent past behind. Mandalore's leader, Duchess Satine, often uses the ship to meet with planetary leaders and Senators

## DATA FILE

**MANUFACTURER:** Kalevala Spaceworks

**MODEL:** Custom Luxury Spaceliner

**CLASS:** Transport

**HEIGHT:** 215.77m (707.9ft)

**CREW:** 75

**WEAPONS:** Laser Cannons, Ion Cannons

**AFFILIATION:** Private

## Exotic Ports of Call

THE *CORONET* INCREASINGLY carries Republic tourists curious about Mandalore and its neighbors—planets they know only from lurid holodramas about ancient warriors. Mandalorian officials and entrepreneurs also take advantage of the liner's frequent runs between Mandalorian space and the galaxy's Core Worlds.

FRONT SIDE VIEW

### Just in Case
The *Coronet* is a luxury vessel, and Satine loathes violence of any form. But a liner carrying rich passengers is a tempting target for pirates, and so the *Coronet* is equipped with laser and ion cannons for defense.

### Think About Tomorrow
SATINE HOPES THE *Coronet*'s trips to Coruscant are a sign of better days ahead, with Mandalorians admired in galactic society for their artistry instead of feared for their ancient ways. But she knows the galaxy is at war—and that rogue Mandalorians wish to revive the old warrior codes.

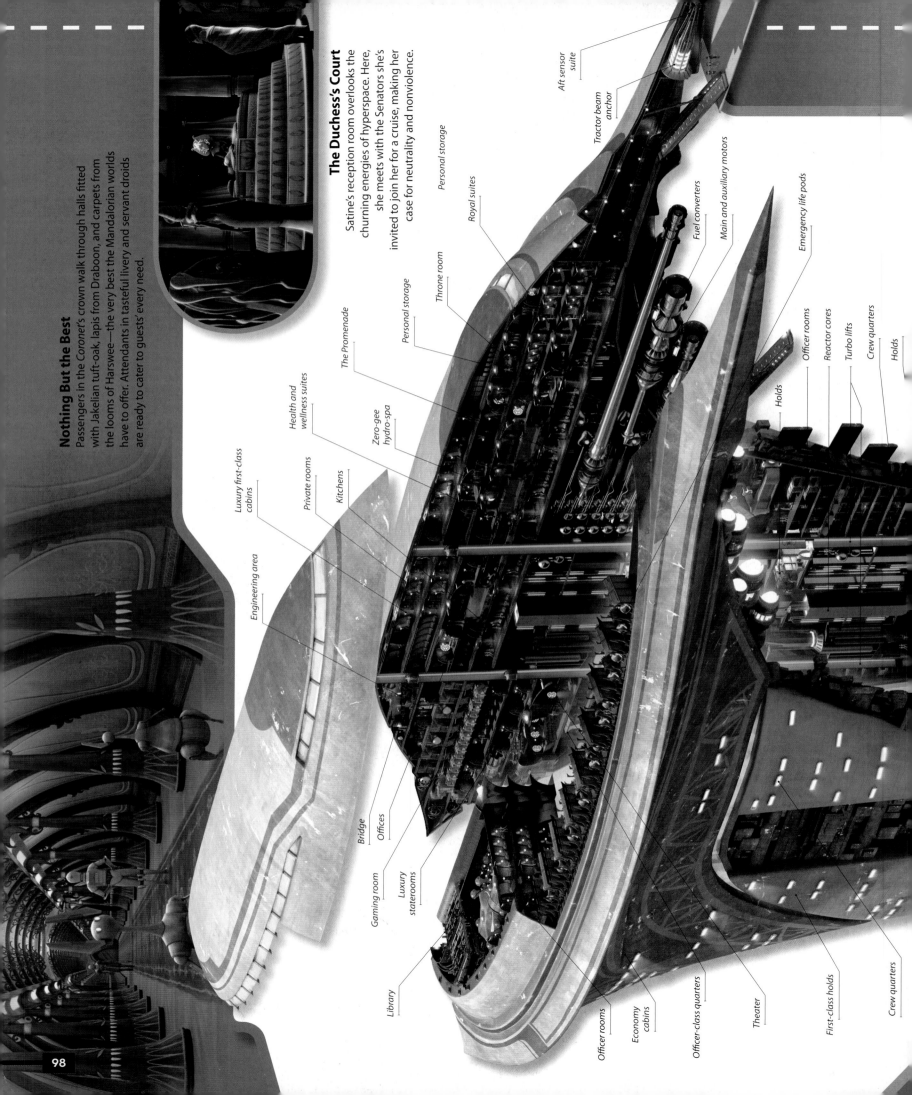

**Nothing But the Best**
Passengers in the Coronet's crown walk through halls fitted with Jakelian tuft-oak, lapis from Draboon, and carpets from the looms of Harswee—the very best the Mandalorian worlds have to offer. Attendants in tasteful livery and servant droids are ready to cater to guests' every need.

**The Duchess's Court**
Satine's reception room overlooks the churning energies of hyperspace. Here, she meets with the Senators she's invited to join her for a cruise, making her case for neutrality and nonviolence.

Aft sensor suite

Tractor beam anchor

Personal storage

Royal suites

Throne room

Personal storage

The Promenade

Health and wellness suites

Zero-gee hydro-spa

Kitchens

Private rooms

Luxury first-class cabins

Engineering area

Library

Gaming room

Offices

Bridge

Luxury staterooms

Fuel converters

Main and auxiliary motors

Emergency life pods

Holds

Officer rooms

Reactor cores

Turbo lifts

Crew quarters

Holds

Officer rooms

Economy cabins

Officer-class quarters

Theater

First-class holds

Crew quarters

# INSIDE THE
# *Coronet*

THE *CORONET* IS simultaneously an elegant vessel for the galaxy's wealthy and a utilitarian craft carrying trade goods and passengers seeking cheap passage. Its richly appointed crown features banquet halls and luxurious staterooms, while its lower spine contains simple quarters and cargo decks.

## At the Helm
On the *Coronet's* bridge, Captain Gray supervises the efforts of his crew. The helmsman stands at a wooden wheel reminiscent of an ancient Kalevalan sea-galley.

*Crew quarters*

*Massive power trunking*

*Laser and ion cannons*

*Holds*

*Cooling fins*

*Repulsor projectors*

*Ventral bridge*

## Separatist Attack
Rogue Mandalorians allied with the Separatists attack the *Coronet* in Droch boarding ships, sending terrified passengers fleeing for the lifeboats.

*Cargo holds*

## Banquet for VIPs
Satine's banquet for the Senators is about to be gate-crashed by an uninvited guest: an assassin probe climbing the turbolift from the cargo decks far below.

## In the Spine
LUXURY TRAVEL ALONE can't pay the operating expenses of a liner the size of the *Coronet*. The great ship's lower decks are mostly for cargo, stockpiling goods shipped through Mandalore for delivery to the worlds in the center of the galaxy.

## Traveling Light
The *Coronet's* lower decks include economy cabins for travelers on a budget. As Jedi, Obi-Wan and Anakin refuse luxury quarters, sharing a basic cabin instead.

# NABOO STAR YACHT

THIS SLIM, NEEDLE-NOSED star yacht is part of the fleet belonging to the Royal House of Naboo. One was lent to Padmé Amidala when she accompanied Anakin Skywalker to Tatooine, and has remained on loan to her for use on Senate business, and for the occasional quick trip back to her beloved homeworld.

*Aerodynamic shape boosts atmospheric speed*

*Projector modules for deflector shield*

*Trio of high-tension landing skids*

## Fit for Royalty

NABOO TRADITION RESERVES the chromium plating of this star yacht for the Royal House, and Padmé gave up her crown years ago. However, an exception has been made out of gratitude for her service to Naboo.

## DATA FILE

MANUFACTURER: Theed Palace Space Vessel Engineering Corps

MODEL: Customized H-type Nubian Yacht

CLASS: Transport

LENGTH: 37.56m (122.58ft)

CREW: 2 to 4

WEAPONS: None

AFFILIATION: Naboo

# NABOO STAR SKIFF

AS A NABOO ROYAL ship, this star skiff shares the chromium finish of the star yacht, but it offers a bat-winged silhouette instead of the yacht's elegant teardrop shape. Like the yacht, the star skiff's primary use is a passenger transport, but its engines have been modified for greater speed, and recent upgrades have seen weapons added.

## DATA FILE

MANUFACTURER: Theed Palace Space Vessel Engineering Corps

MODEL: Customized J-type Nubian Star Skiff

CLASS: Transport

LENGTH: 28.76m (94.33ft)

CREW: 3

WEAPONS: Laser Cannons

AFFILIATION: Naboo

## Changing Times

BECAUSE OF THE peaceful role of Naboo Royal starships, it would once have been unthinkable for such craft to carry weapons. But these are not ordinary times and laser cannons now protrude from the hull, marring the ship's elegant lines.

*Twin laser cannons controlled from cockpit*

*Power regulators and access grilles for new engines*

*Engine nacelles are discolored because of deferred maintenance*

# STAR SKIFF: RENDEZVOUS ON RODIA

Powerful electromagnets are used in spaceport hangars to move shipping containers from place to place. Only trained personnel should operate these heavy magnets—they can do considerable damage if mishandled.

To Chancellor Palpatine's displeasure, Padmé visits Rodia in her personal vessel, accompanied only by Representative Jar Jar Binks and C-3PO. Padmé argues that bringing clone troopers as escorts would be a poor way to begin a peace mission.

When Jar Jar hits the wrong lever (again), the electromagnet crashes into the skiff just forward of the cockpit, smashing the graceful hull into scrap and pulverizing the hyperdrive.

# Diplomatic Mission

PADMÉ AMIDALA VISITS the embattled world of Rodia aboard her star skiff, hoping to convince her old friend Onaconda Farr to end his flirtation with the Separatists. But Nute Gunray has brought his battle droids to the swamp world to capture Padmé—and as if that weren't danger enough, Padmé is accompanied by clumsy Jar Jar Binks.

The skiff's communications array is undamaged by the accident with the electromagnet, but C-3PO discovers that the power feeds have been severed. The golden droid will have to find another transmitter to summon help.

Most starship captains shut their vessels up tight while in spaceports, but diplomatic visits such as Padmé's demand demonstrations of trust, such as leaving ramps down.

# *Flarestar* Attack Shuttle

HONDO OWNS SEVERAL of these saucer-shaped attack shuttles. When they aren't being used to ambush passing ships or raid lawless worlds, they ride in the belly of the much larger frigate, the *Acushnet*.

Dual cockpit design

## DATA FILE

MANUFACTURER: Haor Chall Engineering

MODEL: *Flarestar*-class Attack Shuttle

CLASS: Shuttle

DIAMETER: 22.56m (74ft)

CREW: 3

WEAPONS: Laser Cannons, Torpedo Launchers

AFFILIATION: Varies

**Good Help is Hard to Find**
*Flarestars* can outmaneuver most civilian craft when flown by good pilots. Unfortunately, Hondo doesn't have many of those: Most of his gang are mere thugs.

Emblem of Hondo's pirate gang

Dual thrusters operate in aerial and space modes

Ball turrets allow wide firing arcs

# HONDO'S NAVY

HONDO OHNAKA'S NAVY is a grab bag of ships bought on the cheap or stolen from unlucky travelers, along with tanks and speeder bikes that Hondo swiped from his former master Porla the Hutt.

## DATA FILE

MANUFACTURER: Ikas-Adno

MODEL: Starhawk Speeder Bike

CLASS: Speeder Bike

LENGTH: 3.42m (11.2ft)

CREW: 1 to 3

WEAPONS: Laser Cannons (on some models)

AFFILIATION: Varies

*Decorations added by bored, artistic pirates*

*Optional sidecar*

## Starhawk Speeder Bike

HONDO'S RAIDERS LOVE racing into a village on their battered Starhawk swoops and terrorizing their victims. Some of the two-man bikes have laser cannons while others are fitted with energy couplers for towing cargo.

### Bragging Rights
Running a pirate gang involves plenty of headaches: Hondo constantly has to break up pirate fights over who gets to drive a Starhawk, who takes the rear seat, and who gets stuck riding in the sidecar.

### SEE ALSO

**PIRATE TANK**
Pages 108–111

**HONDO'S FRIGATE**
*ACUSHNET*
Page 78

The front airscoop feeds the turbojet engine, in which a fuel mix is ignited, producing exhaust, a considerable amount of thrust, and a lot of noise due to impellers that are in need of maintenance.

Power feeds terminate in attachment points for antipersonnel blaster cannons. Most of Hondo's Starhawks lack onboard cannons, with the pirates wielding their own pistols and rifles instead.

# STARHAWK SPEEDER BIKE: PIRATE ATTACK ON FLORRUM

The Starhawk's front forks are protected by a stiff cowling, with the bike's steering vanes built into a foot that also includes the front repulsorlift array. This makes the bike stiff but very steady in transit.

# Riding To War

AFTER A REPUBLIC shuttle carrying strongboxes full of credits crashes on the plains of Florrum, Hondo Ohnaka's lieutenant Turk Falso leads a gang of pirates to the crash site on Starhawk speeder bikes. The noisy bikes are easy to control, stable enough to fire weapons from, and equipped with energy couplers for pulling cargo behind them.

The Starhawk's control yoke is rugged, simple, and easy to control. Swoop racers and tinkerers dislike Starhawks for their sluggish steering, but Hondo's bikes are built to be tough and reliable, not flashy. A sturdy control yoke also means a pirate can take a hand off to fire his blaster.

The Starhawk's rear repulsorlifts give it three points of balance, making the bike slow to turn but stable. The oversized repulsorlifts keep the bike from tipping backwards when towing cargo.

## Porla's Property

HONDO'S COLLECTION OF Ubrikkian pirate tanks once belonged to Porla the Hutt, a crimelord from the Boonta. Hondo and many of his pirates once served Porla, but when they decided to strike out on their own, they helped themselves to some of the Hutt gangster's tanks.

## DATA FILE

MANUFACTURER: Ubrikkian Ord Pedrovia

MODEL: WLO-5 Speeder Tank

CLASS: Repulsorcraft

LENGTH: 11.47m (37.6ft)

CREW: 3

WEAPONS: Laser Cannon

AFFILIATION: Varies

# PIRATE TANK

PIRATES GET WHAT they want by taking it—and the easiest way to take something is to have a bigger gun than the other guy. Whether defending their base on Florrum or raiding remote planets, Hondo Ohnaka's gang relies on their fleet of Ubrikkian tanks, which let them outgun most things, even some planetary authorities.

## Beware Gungans

ON FLORRUM, THE pirate Turk Falso leads several tanks onto the plains to confront Jar Jar Binks and his clone troopers. The Gungan is hopelessly outgunned, but Jar Jar causes so much chaos that he winds up defeating the pirates.

FRONT SIDE VIEW

### Armed and Dangerous

A smart pirate doesn't take chances: If Hondo expects opposition, he backs up his tanks with air cover from his *Flarestar* attack shuttles and sends out skirmishers on Starhawk speeder bikes.

## At the Controls

The WLO-5's driver relies on a bank of visual scanners as well as whatever can be seen through the tank's narrow portals. The controls are so simple that even a Kowakian monkey-lizard can drive it—though that's not a good idea.

**Thrust chamber**

**Plasma energy belt**

**Fuel ionization system**

**Fuel tank**

**Starboard turbines**

**Power generator**

**Power converters**

**Power feeds**

### Motivated Sellers

THE DESIGN OF the WLO-5 is similar to that of several other tanks: Ubrikkian is controlled by the Hutts, who feel no shame about stealing ideas from competitors. Ubrikkian isn't picky about whom it sells to. Local governments, pirates, smugglers, or almost anyone else can buy a WLO-5, as long as they have the credits.

**Adjustable cooling vane**

**Power generator heat vents**

**Hinge for cooling vane**

**Access hatch**

**Steering vane**

**Steering control linkages**

**Damaged repulsorlift heat sink**

**Steering switching mechanism**

**Radiator grille**

# INSIDE THE
# Pirate Tank

THE WLO-5 LACKS missiles that can take out heavy armor or fortified emplacements, but it is easily a match for light tanks or small fighting vehicles. It is fast enough for skirmishing, and its armor provides protection for troops being ferried into battle. Besides, pirates rarely pick fights with those who can fight back.

### Pirate Philosophy

Life has taught Hondo that the galaxy is a cruel place, and a wise being grabs what profits he can in what time he's given. Hondo says the best way to do that is to "speak softly and drive a big tank!"

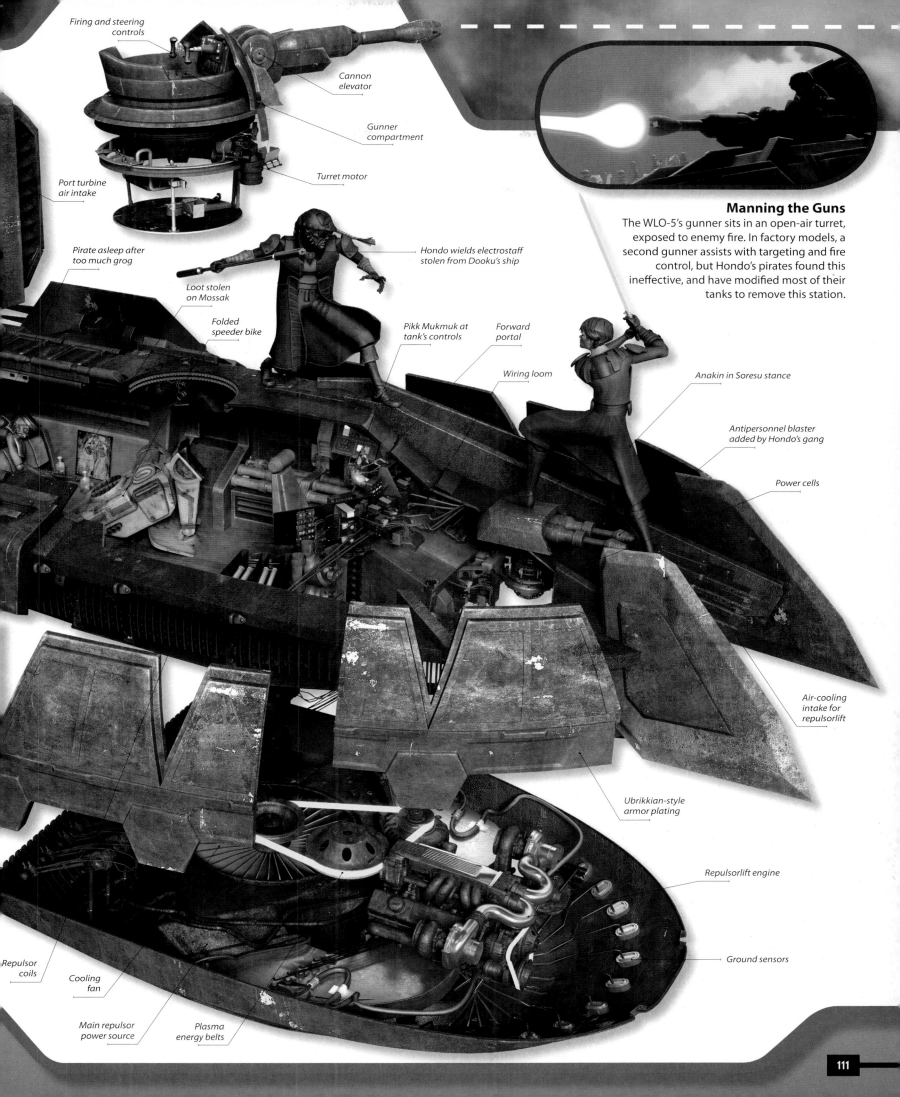

Firing and steering controls

Cannon elevator

Gunner compartment

Turret motor

Port turbine air intake

Pirate asleep after too much grog

Loot stolen on Mossak

Folded speeder bike

Hondo wields electrostaff stolen from Dooku's ship

Pikk Mukmuk at tank's controls

Forward portal

Wiring loom

Anakin in Soresu stance

Antipersonnel blaster added by Hondo's gang

Power cells

Air-cooling intake for repulsorlift

Ubrikkian-style armor plating

Repulsorlift engine

Ground sensors

Repulsor coils

Cooling fan

Main repulsor power source

Plasma energy belts

## Manning the Guns
The WLO-5's gunner sits in an open-air turret, exposed to enemy fire. In factory models, a second gunner assists with targeting and fire control, but Hondo's pirates found this ineffective, and have modified most of their tanks to remove this station.

# TRANDOSHAN HUNT SHIP

*THE VERMIN-THRAX* began its life as an anonymous bulk freighter, hopping between industrial spaceports. It has since been modified by the Trandoshan Garnac to accommodate a new type of cargo—prisoners. These unlucky captives are transported to the moon Wasskah, where they are released and hunted for sport.

## DATA FILE

MANUFACTURER: Gallofree Yards

MODEL: Modified HCT-2001 *Dragonboat*-class Freighter

CLASS: Freighter

LENGTH: 95.28m (312.58ft)

CREW: 2

WEAPONS: Rotary Laser Cannon

AFFILIATION: Trandoshans

## Prison Ship

GARNAC CONVERTED THE freighter's extensive cargo modules into slave pens that drop open to release prisoners. In light of the ship's new dark role, Garnac also outfitted it with a chin turret and blaster.

*Cargo modules refitted to hold prisoners*

*Flight deck in the rear, far from the cargo decks*

*Main engines with rear breaking thrusters*

# TRANDOSHAN HOVER POD

HOVER PODS ARE designed for planetary scouts, allowing the driver and observers excellent visibility over the ground below. They have also proved popular for recreational safaris. The Trandoshan hover pod, however, is uniquely used for a darker purpose.

## Rough and Ready

QUICK AND FAST, hover pods are ideal for chasing prisoners through the jungles of Wasskah. Three hunters fit in each pod. They play for sport, scanning the trees, sniffing the air, and waiting for an unwary victim to wander into the crosshairs of their blasters.

## DATA FILE

MANUFACTURER: Gallofree Aerial Products

MODEL: MSP80 Pteropter Hover Pod

CLASS: Airspeeder

LENGTH: 4.11m (13.5ft)

CREW: 1 to 3

WEAPONS: Rotary Blaster Cannon, Laser Cannons

AFFILIATION: Trandoshans

*Rotary cannon controlled by driver*

# TRANDOSHAN HOVER POD: CRUEL SPORT ON WASSKAH

Cylinders on the back of the pods hold rifles, stun guns, and net launchers so the hunters have their hands free in flight. A mild tractor field keeps guns from falling out.

Hover pods' headlamps are powerful enough to cut through the darkness, and cast light across the infrared and ultraviolet ends of the spectrum.

A screen of steel mesh on the front of each pod prevents fugitives or wildlife from launching frontal attacks on the hunters.

The Trandoshans' Ubrikkian floating fortress serves as their home base, hanging in the sky cruelly far out of reach of any fugitive dreaming of taking revenge on the hunters.

Each pod has winches to lever itself out of trouble or pull another pod free if it gets stuck. Cables can also be used to carry prey for display as trophies of a successful hunt.

# The Hunt Is On!

WHEN THE SUN rises on Wasskah, it's time for the Hunt to begin. Garnac's Trandoshan hunters leave their floating fortress in their hover pods, swooping down on the islands below to hunt the captives they dropped on the beach the night before. Fugitives who hope to survive the deadly hunt learn to listen for the whine of a pod's repulsorlift and hide deep in the jungle.

### Back to Basics

THE HALO IS a capable gunship, with
cannons offering a near-360-degree field of
fire, impressive maneuverability, and landing
gear designed to withstand the shock of
a hard touchdown. On Wasskah, Wookiee
warriors descend drop lines with the kind
of precision that would make clones proud.

### False Advertising

Botajef Shipyards designed the SS-54 as an attack
ship for Planetary Security Forces, but a suspicious
clerical error led to the craft's misclassification as a
light freighter. As a result, many were sold without
proper clearance by Republic authorities.

**Going Vertical**

THE HALO'S OVERSIZED engines rotate to a vertical orientation for takeoffs and landings, though the craft can also launch and land in flight mode.

## DATA FILE

**MANUFACTURER:** Botajef Shipyards

**MODEL:** SS-54 Assault Ship

**CLASS:** Gunship

**LENGTH:** 24.19m (79.4ft)

**CREW:** 3

**WEAPONS:** Laser Cannons

**AFFILIATION:** Sugi

# HALO

THE BOUNTY HUNTER Sugi is the captain of the *Halo*, an assault ship that she and her band of mercenaries use on missions across the galaxy. The *Halo* bristles with laser cannons and boasts two massive turbine engines, giving it impressive speed and demonstrating that its owner is not someone to mess with. To make that message crystal-clear, a knife-wielding Tooka doll adorns the ship's nose, along with the message, "Nice Playing With Ya."

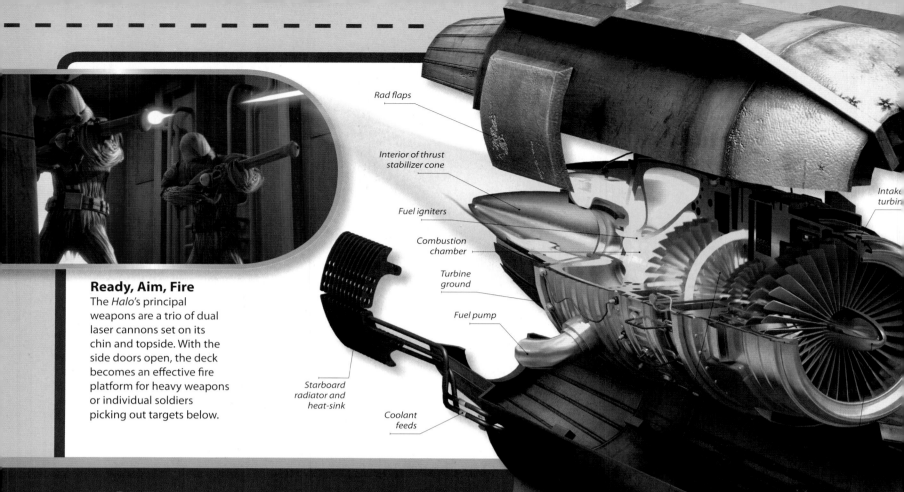

Rad flaps

Interior of thrust
stabilizer cone

Fuel igniters

Combustion
chamber

Turbine
ground

Fuel pump

Intake
turbine

Starboard
radiator and
heat-sink

Coolant
feeds

Compressor

Drive motor
nacelle

### Ready, Aim, Fire

The *Halo*'s principal weapons are a trio of dual laser cannons set on its chin and topside. With the side doors open, the deck becomes an effective fire platform for heavy weapons or individual soldiers picking out targets below.

# INSIDE THE
# *Halo*

SUGI'S CONVERTED GUNSHIP is a workhorse, effective as a speedy transport for getting her band of mercenaries in and out of trouble spots as well as for raking enemies with gunfire in lightning-quick aerial assaults. The *Halo* is also small enough to tuck away in a warehouse, barn, or forest clearing—useful since a lethal-looking gunship tends to attract attention sitting among freighters and transports at a spaceport.

### Rough and Ready

IN ITS FACTORY configuration, the *Halo* was built for strike missions launched from a carrier or base. However, in refitting it to a longer-range craft, Sugi added a crew cabin, refresher, space for supplies, and converted the gunship's stern hold. But even with such alterations, the *Halo* isn't exactly a luxury craft: Passengers feel the thrum of her engines and every bump and bounce of travel. Which is how Sugi likes it.

### Flying Visit

After rescuing Ahsoka and her fellow Padawans from Wasskah, Sugi agrees to return them to Coruscant. But she keeps the *Halo*'s engines warm: The Republic authorities don't approve of guns for hire, even when they help Jedi.

**Honor and Duty (and Credits)**
Sugi abides by a code of ethics, refusing to switch sides for more credits or quit a job even in the face of danger. But she doesn't work for free—and as she warns Tarfful, customers are responsible for any damage to her ship.

Rear blaster cannon

Gunners' station

Engine nozzle

Primary portside power cell

Port turbojet radiator

Heat vent

Power regulators

120-degree rotational ball joint

Turbine cowling

Starboard generator

Starboard fuel tank

Main reactor

Energy storage reservoirs

Cabin atmosphere mixer

Life-support modules

Ladder to troop hold

Sensor displays

Cockpit

Sugi

Obi-Wan Kenobi

Ahsoka Tano

Rumi Paramita's body

Side door

Short-range sensors

Shock-absorbent landing gear

Seripas

Embo

Anakin Skywalker

Power conduit channel

Cannon power converter and capacitor arrays

Rapid-recharge power cells

Landing gear power feeds

Cannon heat-sink

Chin laser cannons

Terrain-following sensor suite

# SHUTTLECRAFT

SHUTTLES ARE DEPLOYED for transporting small numbers of personnel in situations where capital ships would be slow or inconvenient. Some shuttles carry troops and are armed; others rely only on speed or robust shields to keep their passengers safe.

## T-6 Shuttle

THIS SPEEDY JEDI shuttle has a gyroscopic cockpit set on shock-resistant gimbals. This means that it remains upright during flight maneuvers, helping to keep pilots oriented if they must take evasive action.

*Rotating wing in vertical position for maneuvers*

**Verpine Engineering**
The T-6 was built for the Jedi Order by the Verpine hives of the Roche system, though other elites on Coruscant now fly them too. The ship benefits from the insectoid race's extensive technological tinkering, with swing-wing designs, gyroscopic cockpits, and other starship innovations.

## DATA FILE

MANUFACTURER: Slayn & Korpil

MODEL: T-6 Shuttle

CLASS: Shuttle

LENGTH: 22.8m (74.8ft)

CREW: 2, plus passengers

WEAPONS: None

AFFILIATION: Varies

## DATA FILE

MANUFACTURER: Slayn & Korpil

MODEL: H-2 Executive Shuttle

CLASS: Shuttle

LENGTH: 14.63m (48ft)

CREW: 1

WEAPONS: None

AFFILIATION: Varies

*Reinforced armor protects cockpit and crew cabin*

*Turbojets designed for rapid startup*

# Executive Shuttle

THE EXECUTIVE SHUTTLE is made for peacetime transportation so it lacks shielding. Supreme Chancellor Palpatine keeps a pair close at hand for travels on Coruscant, whose skies are well-defended by Republic military units and the airspeeders of the Senate Guard.

# *Eta*-class Shuttle

DESIGNED FOR TRANSPORTING important ambassadors and political leaders, the *Eta* shuttle sports enhanced shielding and a suite of sensor-jamming technology.

*Tri-winged design is a Cygnus hallmark*

*"Bubble" cockpit gives pilot maximum visibility*

## SEE ALSO

**MANDOLORIAN SHUTTLE**
Page 94

***NU*-CLASS ATTACK SHUTTLE**
Page 123

***SHEATHIPEDE* SHUTTLE**
Page 122

## DATA FILE

MANUFACTURER: Cygnus Spaceworks

MODEL: *Eta*-class Shuttle

CLASS: Shuttle

LENGTH: 14.15m (46.4ft)

CREW: 2

WEAPONS: Laser Cannons

AFFILIATION: Republic

# SHEATHIPEDE SHUTTLE

THE SHEATHIPEDE IS the shuttle of choice for wealthy Neimoidians on business trips. Its luxurious interior is designed to help passengers forget they are traveling at all as they relax in a sumptuous salon. To reinforce this idea, the pilots are screened off from the cabin. On some models the cockpit is removed entirely and replaced by autopilots to increase cabin space.

## DATA FILE

MANUFACTURER: Haor Chall Engineering

MODEL: *Sheathipede*-class Shuttle

CLASS: Shuttle

LENGTH: 14.44m (47.42ft)

CREW: 1

WEAPONS: Laser Cannons (optional)

AFFILIATION: Separatists

Armored cabin for passengers

## The Price of War

AS THE CLONE Wars tore the galaxy apart, Trade Federation officials equipped their shuttles with advanced shields, laser cannons, and other concessions to the realities of war.

Armed shuttles have trio of laser cannons

Landing struts resemble a beetle's clawed legs

# NU-CLASS ATTACK SHUTTLE

REPUBLIC STRATEGISTS imagined the *Nu*-class shuttle as a troop transport, swooping in with cannons blazing to deliver clone troopers to the front lines. While the Nu is effective on such missions, it is also often used as a personal transport for high-ranking Republic officers, senators, and Jedi.

## DATA FILE

MANUFACTURER: Cygnus Spaceworks

MODEL: *Nu*-class Attack Shuttle

CLASS: Shuttle

LENGTH: 24.34m (79.9ft)

CREW: 2

WEAPONS: Laser Cannons

AFFILIATION: Republic

Boarding ramp positioned to be covered by guns

Fold-down wings rotate upward for takeoff and landing

## Gunship Support

AS A SPEEDIER, longer-range support to the Republic gunship, the Nu shuttle is faster and incorporates some of the gunship's features, such as ball turrets. But it can't match the gunship's field of fire or cargo capacity.

No fewer than six laser cannons defend the Nu's boarding ramp, and clones note that it's one of the safest places in the galaxy. Unfortunately, few missions allow troopers to stay where they're protected by the guns.

Military vehicles get priority in the crowded skies of Coruscant: With the shuttle nearly ready for liftoff, the traffic lanes have been pushed even farther away from the Jedi Temple than usual.

# Off to War!

THE *NU-CLASS* attack shuttle is a standard transport for Jedi and clones on Clone Wars business for the Republic. When Anakin and Captain Rex are ordered to war-torn Balith to take charge of the Third Legion, Ahsoka is unhappy to find herself left behind, but still sees them off from the landing pad at the Jedi Temple.

The Nu's cockpit is positioned so the pilot can easily survey the terrain directly in front of the nose. This is essential to ensure troops don't disembark and find themselves in a poor strategic position.

As Anakin says farewell to his Padawan, Rex and another trooper of Torrent Company prepare to take their seats in the troop hold inside the shuttle's well-armored belly.

The Nu's landing gear can be adjusted to sit low to the ground, allowing clone troopers to rush down a gently inclined ramp. Here, the Jedi Temple is a safe place, so the gear is set high for easier loading and maintenance.

# INDEX

LONDON, NEW YORK, MELBORNE, MUNICH, AND DELHI

For Dorling Kindersley
**SENIOR EDITOR:** Elizabeth Dowsett
**ADDITIONAL EDITORS:** Emma Grange,
Lisa Stock, Victoria Taylor
**DESIGNER:** Toby Truphet
**DESIGN ASSISTANT:** Rhys Thomas
**DESIGN MANAGER:** Ron Stobbart
**PUBLISHING MANAGER:** Catherine Saunders
**ART DIRECTOR:** Lisa Lanzarini
**PUBLISHER:** Simon Beecroft
**PUBLISHING DIRECTOR:** Alex Allan
**PRODUCTION EDITOR:** Siu Chan
**PRODUCTION CONTROLLER:** Nick Seston

Additonal design for Dorling Kindersley
by Dan Bunyan and Lisa Sodeau

For Lucasfilm
**EXECUTIVE EDITOR:** J. W. Rinzler
**ART DIRECTOR:** Troy Alders
**KEEPER OF THE HOLOCRON:** Leland Chee
**DIRECTOR OF PUBLISHING:** Carol Roeder

Dorling Kindersley and Lucasfilm would like to
thank Richard Chasemore for his cross-section
illustrations and Jason Fry for the text.

First published in the United States in 2011
by DK Publishing
375 Hudson Street, New York, New York 10014

11 12 13 14 15  10 9 8 7 6 5 4 3
004-177931-08/2011

Published in Great Britain by Dorling Kindersley Limited.

A catalog record for this book is available from the Library
of Congress.

ISBN: 978-0-7566-8691-8

Color reproduction by Media Development Printing, UK
Printed in China by Hung Hing Printing Group Limited

Discover more at
www.dk.com
www.starwars.com